Wanted by You

A. Boss

PEAK EVEREST PUBLISHING

For all of us who fell in love with a grumpy, blue-collar man.

"To the moon and back."

One.

Cassidy

"Do it, do it, do it." Alison, my coworker and best friend, bounces beside me as I start the early morning brew.

I shake my head. "I'm not writing that on his cup. I meant it as a joke."

She laughs. "And it'll be even funnier when you write it on his cup and give it to him. You *have* to do it, Cassidy."

I've worked here at Cup O' Joe for almost three years. The simple, small-town favorite coffee house. Serving the best coffee in Montana, if you ask me. "I'm not writing *Smile, Asshole* on Butch Montgomery's to-go cup. It's not happening. And don't even try writing it, your handwriting sucks. He'll know it was you, not me."

"Good morning, girls." Peggy sings, shuffling through the front door with her usual morning bundle of baked goods for the display.

Peggy Cup, my boss and owner of Cup O' Joe, is the sweetest, kindest woman I've ever known. She named the quaint place after her late husband, Joe. Unfortunately, he passed away last year, but that's only meant Peggy's been pouring her entire heart and soul into her business.

And it shows. Everything here is *amazing*.

There are three of us lead shift ladies who work for Peggy. Myself, Alison, and Janice—along with a few part-time high schoolers. Since this is Alison's second job, she only works for the first three hours each morning. Making up a load of breakfast sandwiches and helping me or Janice with the morning rush.

As an old friend of Peggy's, Janice does this for something to do since her husband got injured working on the mountain. She swears she's only here to get away from his complaining and their four kids still living at home. But secretly, she loves the town gossip and having a few laughs with all of us.

Peggy's probably the best boss in the entire world. She *always* rotates weekends and makes sure we each receive at least two days off a week. And when we're open seven days a week, working anytime from 5:00 AM to 3:00 PM, I'm happy for my recovery days.

But what I love most about Peggy is she lets me write while I work. I create and write greeting cards as an active hobby. The artwork, the messages—it's all me.

I've had several greeting card companies purchase my work, but the biggest hands down was *Hallmark*. I nearly *died* when they bought one exclusively from me last year, and I've been *dying* to make another they'll love just as much.

So, I practice at work, trying out little quips and messages on the to-go cups. It started as a fun tease I did for Peggy one day when she was feeling down about Joe. She loved it enough to ask me to start doing it daily for customers. She even gave me a whole dollar raise and bought me a slew of colored Sharpies.

I love it. The customers read them out loud, smile, and tell me thank you. Some even tell me how the message resonates with them. Everyone loves it.

Well, everyone except one person...Butch Montgomery.

The town asshole.

And that's not just my opinion, he's well known for his broody attitude and dire need for anger management. Yet, somehow, every woman wants him—or one of his brothers.

I don't blame them; they're all *men*.

The Montgomery brothers might as well run this town. Each one of them owns a business here in our small community. They get plenty of respect from everyone—not that their egos need it, mind you. It might as well be changed from Whitetail, Montana to *Montgomery*, Montana.

But Butch... He's a man's man. Standing at six-foot-six with broad, hulking shoulders and large, calloused hands. He's a wet dream in a deep red button-down flannel, dirty jeans, and work boots. All man and no bullshit—*literally*.

One morning, when I gave him his routine, extra-large black coffee to-go, I used one that had a few doodled flowers on it. They were just flowers! The man had a bitch fit, saying he asked for a black coffee, not a black doodled flower on his cup.

The audacity of this man, I swear.

I swore right then and there, he would *never* get a welcome, good morning, doodle, or sweet message on his cup from me again. I can take criticism, but this wasn't criticism. It was blatant asshole-ory, and I have no room in my life for his Negative Nancy energy.

I've got enough of it already weighing me down.

"Peggy," Alison beams, rushing around the counter to help her bring everything in. "Tell Cassidy she should write *Smile, Asshole* on Butch's coffee this morning. Please!"

Our boss laughs heartily. "Oh, that's a good one. Very fitting."

Alison spins around, her eyes lit up like a Christmas tree. "See. You have to do it now."

I shake my head. "Don't encourage her, Peggy. I meant it as a joke."

Peggy smiles, coming in with a large tray of assorted cookies for the display. "Well, I love it. He'll probably get a kick out of it. More than the flower cup you gave him last time."

I scoff. "That flower cup was stunning, one of the best roses I've ever drawn was on that cup. And you know what he did? He tossed the entire thing in the trash—didn't even take a sip from it! Demanded a new coffee, took it, and stomped off in his boots like some caveman."

"Okay, you really need to let that go. It's been six months," Alison tells me, helping Peggy stock the display.

"All the more reason to put this on his cup." Peggy chuckles. "And as your boss, I'm telling you to do it."

I cross my arms over my chest, standing my ground. "I'm not doing it."

Alison giggles as Peggy turns to me, raising a very serious brow. "Cassidy Clark, I gave you a raise to do exactly what I'm telling you to do now. Don't you sass me, young lady. Now, grab an extra-large to-go cup and Sharpie, and get to fancy writing. I want the 'A' in asshole to be capitalized."

Alison booms with laughter, high-fiving Peggy. "This is going to be *so* good."

Like a scolded child, I do as I'm told, grabbing a cup and Sharpie. "Fine, but when he slashes my tires or keys my car, I'll be blaming both of you," I say, examining the cup for the best place to write this where he won't notice it until he's long gone from the coffee shop.

And then it clicks. *Ha!*

Alison comes back around the counter. "Oh, come on, he'll never see it there."

Peggy glances over with a smile on her face. "Always such a smartass, Cassidy."

I smile brightly, setting the cup off to the side that now has *Smile, Asshole* written on the bottom of it. "Hey, I'm just doing what you pay me to do." I wink, watching as one of our early morning regulars shuffles through the front door.

"Morning, ladies." Wade nods toward the counter with his morning paper in hand. "I'll have my usual." He takes his time getting to his favorite spot beside the front window.

"Coming right up, Wade," I call, getting his coffee and breakfast sandwich.

Since we only use the to-go cups for to-go orders, everything here is served in mugs and on dessert plates. So Peggy has me write my messages on a small napkin to be taken with each order.

Gathering up Wade's order and a napkin from the little stockpile I have going, I walk over and place it down in front of him. He smiles, handing me cash to pay his bill. As I make my way back around to the register, he reads the napkin message out loud.

"*It doesn't matter how slow you go, as long as you don't stop,*" Wade chuckles deeply. "Love it, Cassidy. I'll tell ya what, I'm feelin' slow today."

"Oh, I like that one," Peggy chimes brightly.

I smile. "Peggy, you say that about all my little one-liners."

She huffs, giving me a sassy side-eye of her own. "And I mean it. Now quit being such a sass and get me my coffee, please. I'll be in the back office for a bit this morning."

I snicker to myself, turning to retrieve her request. Alison heads to the kitchen to finish whipping up the dozens of breakfast sandwiches we go through each day. The early morning rush starts, and it's not long before I glance at the clock, 6:07 AM. The bell above the door rings, and I don't even need to look to know it's him.

Here we go.

Reaching over—and against all my better judgment—I grab the extra-large to-go cup with the *loveliest* message written on the bottom. Turning back to the counter, I place the black coffee down in front of a towering, scowling Butch Montgomery.

With his strong jaw ticking, eyes dark, and brows furrowed for extra scowling flare, you'd think he was in his forties when he's only thirty-four. The trimmed beard he has is a dark, chestnut brown, matching his shorter, slicked-back hair.

I bet he buys his neon work shirts a size *too* small just to get the attention he supposedly *hates* from all the women in town.

I hold back a snort at the thought.

"Extra-large black coffee, two breakfast sandwiches, and a chocolate chunk cookie. To go," he grumbles. His voice comes out deep and dark with a growling rasp. Tossing cash on the counter in front of me, he stares down at his phone without paying me a second glance.

Always the gentleman. *Not.*

I roll my eyes. It's not like he'll see it anyway.

Getting his order, I place it all neatly in a paper bag, putting it beside his coffee. And as he always does, he grabs it and goes. Not even giving me a chance to say his total or give him his change.

Tossing the abandoned change in the tip jar, I gaze out the front window. Watching Butch get into his big-ass black truck wrapped in his company's name written in a bold steel and yellow: *Montgomery Logging*. He pulls out and heads down the road toward the mountain, the same as every day.

"Asshole," I curse.

Butch

SHE ROLLED HER EYES at me again today.

That's three days straight, our new record. Wonder if she even knows it.

But hell, if she didn't look beautiful today as always. Those snug black yoga pants, the oversized beige Cup O' Joe work shirt she has to tie in the back just so it doesn't hang droopy around her. And fuck—those curves.

She's got a perfect hourglass figure with an ass that pops. And compared to my broad stature, she can't be more than five-foot-four. Her brown hair, always up in a messy top bun with bits hanging down to frame her face. Those stunning deep blue eyes that I could stare into for eternity under thick black lashes. Plump lips framing a perfect smile—but *god*, those eyes.

Everything about her has me stumbling, I can't even look her in the eye half the fuckin' time. She's drop-dead gorgeous, and either she knows it or has no clue.

Cassidy Clark. The only woman who wants nothing to do with me, and the only one I seem to have eyes for ever since she came back from college three years ago. She's ten years younger than me, one of the many reasons I don't stand a chance. She probably gets men groveling at her feet on the daily.

I've watched her date a few punks around town, but it never seems to last or get serious. And in our small town—population: five thousand, three hundred twenty-seven—word gets around *quick*. It's never long before everyone knows who screwed who, who lost their job, who died, who's pregnant, who cheated on who.

It's why I've been single for the last five years.

Yup, the good ol' grapevine told me my ex was sleeping with some jack-off from a few towns over when she'd go visit "family." Not even a quick fuck outside a fifty-mile radius could stop the gossiping Bettys from catching wind of the scorching hot tea and pouring it all over me.

Bitch broke my heart, so I tossed the ring I got her in the woodchipper.

Burn me once...shame on you, me, and the money wasted.

Montgomery Logging is the company I built from the ground up. Went from nothing to something, and I'm damn proud of it. It got me my property where I built my dream home with my own bare hands, my custom detailed truck, and a solid bank account. One every gold digger in town seems to want to get a piece of. Another prime reason why I'm single.

And it's probably why I want my shot at Cassidy.

She's not like the rest. She left this town, got an education, and only came back when her father got sick and died of cancer a few years back. The gossip line says her mother ran off to California with some tourist she met passing through and no one's heard a word from her since.

Cassidy stayed for her older brother, Garrett. He's a punk himself—drunk as a skunk twenty-four-seven. And while I may be the town asshole, he's the town drunk.

Garrett and I...well, you could say we've had a few quarrels in the past and present. A mutual hate is the kind of relationship we have. He and I have a routine bar fight every few months when he slumps into the pits of his own hell. I swear the first time I was only trying to help the guy out, but it didn't end up that way. He took a shot at me, so I busted his nose and knocked his ass out cold.

Another reason added to the list of: *I don't stand a chance.*

Pulling up to one of my three current logging site locations on the various surrounding mountains of Montana, I park my truck and hop out. Striding over to my crew of half a dozen for this site.

"Morning, boss," Stan, my head foreman and best friend since high school, yawns in greeting.

I grunt, not in the mood in the slightest this morning for friendly banter. I get straight to it, barking out orders and running through the schedule for today. Who's where and who's running what. I take a sip of my coffee, and out of nowhere, Stan bursts out a laugh.

I scowl. "What the fuck is so funny?"

The idiot starts wheezing with laughter as he keels over. My remaining men turn away, starting to snicker to themselves.

"What?" I bark out.

Stan coughs, pointing to my cup in hand. I look it over, and when I lift the cup to check the bottom—I see it. *Smile, Asshole* is written in perfect cursive with a little heart over the 'I' in smile.

I keep my expression stern, but on the inside, I may or may not be smiling.

It's been nearly six months since I made the mistake of talkin' out my ass about Cassidy's flower-doodled cup. The woman can hold a grudge, that's for sure.

I've gone in every morning, Monday through Friday for the last three years since she came back to town and started working at Cup O' Joe.

I used to get a "Good morning" or a "Welcome to Cup O' Joe" with some bullshit message written on the side of my cup when Peggy had her start doing it for all her customers a year ago—but not the last six months. Not since I apparently insulted her to the highest degree. No, now it's eye rolls or long aggravated sighs.

But in my defense, I was having a shit morning that day.

"Tell me you knew that was there," Stan chokes out, wiping away tears of laughter.

"Looks like Cassidy Clark finally found a message that works for ya, boss," Tanner, one of my younger employees who's weaseled his way under Stan's wing, chimes in. "I got one the other day, something about having a *sunny day*, but nothing with a heart."

I grunt, ignoring them both. "Get to work. Nobody leaves until we make quota. And before you say it, I don't give a fuck that it's Friday. So you better get moving."

My crew nods and heads off to work the mountain. Stan pushes his hands in his pockets, smirking like the dipshit he is. "You going to make me ask, or what?"

"Ask me what?" I grumble, playing dumb even though my mind is reeling. I chug down the remaining bit of coffee and reach into the back of my truck to grab my hard hat.

"Don't give me that shit, Butch." He smirks. "What'd you finally do right to get a custom cup from Cassidy?"

"I didn't do shit," I say, and it's the truth. "And I don't think I'd call her writing *asshole* on my cup worthy of something I did right."

Stan shrugs. "Maybe not. But it's better than nothing."

I huff, not bothering to have this conversation with him right now. Stan knows about my secret obsession with Cassidy—not willingly on my part. One night after *a lot* of whiskey at the bar, I opened up about it to him. And as drunk as he was, he hadn't forgotten the next morning. How it's stayed between us and not hit the gossip line back to her, is beyond me.

Or maybe it did, and that's why she still hates me? *Fuck.*

All I want is a damn chance. Maybe take her out to dinner or some romantic bullshit. I know I'm not helping my case any with the quick hookups here and there I bang out at the local bars. Half the time, I go just to see if she's there, but she never is.

Somehow, even in this small town, I can't seem to run into her outside of the coffee shop. I'm a professional guy myself, I wouldn't want my employees trying to pick up a hot date when they should be working. So yeah, that's more or less been my excuse for not trying to get my shot in.

I'm not a shy guy by any means, but I'm not used to making the first move. Women throw themselves at *me*—not the other way around. I'm not a desperate man. You won't catch me on my knees begging for a woman's company. If anything, I might need a stick to pry them the hell off me.

That's probably why I've been named the town asshole by every woman in Whitetail. Not that I mind the title. I usually end up popping off my mouth with some rude remark in hopes they'll get lost. It either ends in them storming off, or they're fucking into it.

A guy can't win when he wants to lose.

And I guess I can't win Cassidy without trying, right? I just need to find my moment. My shot to say more than my morning order to her.

Hell, I might even apologize for the damn flower cup.

Three.

Cassidy

I shake my head at the ridiculous message. Sliding my phone back into my purse, I lock up the front door of the coffee shop and make my way over to my car. Digging for my car keys, a loud beep comes from behind me. I jump, dropping my keys.

I spin around, my heart pounding in my chest as I'm greeted with the unfortunate sight of my brother, Garrett, and his two drinking buddies. All crammed into a rusted-out, two-door pick-up truck.

Garrett may be my older brother by six years, but at thirty, you'd think he was some college frat boy with how much he parties. It's a wonder his liver hasn't given up on him yet. He's six-foot-two, with shaggy brown hair, and a sharp jawline like our father.

He looks so much like him...it pains me to look at him sometimes.

Garrett sticks his head out as I bend down to grab my keys. "Hey, sis, you coming to the bar tonight? They've got some new Saturday margarita special going. I know how you love your tequila."

I sigh, moving to the side of the truck he's shouting at me out of. "What the hell, Garrett? You gave me a damn heart attack." At his obnoxious snort, I frown. He's a child living in a man's body. "And why are you driving? How are you going to get home from the bar?"

He shrugs. "Figured my good little sis will come snatch me up and bring me home to the old double wide when I'm ready."

"Hey, Cass, lookin' good. You doin' anything later?" Alex, my ex-boyfriend, grins smugly. Sending me a suggestive wink that makes me internally gag.

Unfortunately, in a small town, you don't get away from your exes. They just pile up in town, forever to harass you and be there when you don't want them to be.

Exhibit A: Alex is good friends with Garrett. It's been a few years since Alex and I dated, and clearly, the guy can't take a hint. Even though I'm pretty sure he's dating Marissa Finley from two trailers down in the park. He better watch his friendly 'winking.' Marissa will castrate him faster than he can *wink* a second time.

Ignoring Alex, I focus on my brother. "Which bar?"

He smiles, gesturing over his shoulder down the street. "Tavern Nine. They've even got a live band tonight. Should be a good time. Hey, why don't you ask Madison to come? I haven't seen her around in a while."

I scrunch my nose. "Madison and I aren't talking. She's hooking up with Colt."

Madison is—or was, my best friend. And like small-town drama tends to go, she's dating my most recent ex, Colt. The jerk. If I think Butch is an asshole, Colt takes the cake. Worst mistake of my life and a waste of three months. Why Madison is with him is a mind-blowing question I'll never get the answer to.

Garrett whistles lowly. "Damn, Cass, I didn't know. When'd that happen?"

I shrug. "A few months ago. You'd know if you were home any. Which, by the way, I need lot-rent for this month. You stiffed me last month, dick."

"Uh..." he trails off, "I'll hit you later. And hey, I'll save you a seat tonight, might even buy you a margarita."

Some brother he is. "Fuck you, Garrett." I turn back to my car.

He beeps again, making me jump, *again*. I scowl at him as they laugh and pull off down the street. Taking out my phone, I shoot off a text to a few girlfriends to see if they heard about this margarita night.

I don't even know why I'm entertaining the idea. It might be because I have tomorrow off, but there's been plenty of nights where I could've gone out and I didn't. Don't get me wrong, I like to go out with my friends every now and then. I don't even mind traveling solo most nights since I always end up running into someone I know. But that's the problem, I *always* run into someone I know. Between Alex, Colt, and a few other losers who I—for some reason—gave a chance to, I can't seem to get one good night out.

My phone dings like crazy with messages confirming margarita night at Tavern Nine, all of them mentioning something about they *didn't think I'd want to come*. Guess I deserve that one.

I sigh to myself, starting my car and heading to the trusty-rusty trailer located in Whitetail Park, where everyone in town has a little bit of family living.

Parking in front of the single-wide I share with my brother—the same one our father left us when he died. It's a simple two-bedroom, one-bathroom trailer with a small kitchen-dining-living room space all crammed into one. It's not in bad condition. My father put a good amount of work in to keep it up to date, and I do my best to do the same.

But sometimes it's a lot...even for me.

Getting out, I spot a very excited little sausage waiting for me on the porch with a wagging tail and a little pot belly. Smiling, I walk up the few front porch steps. "There's my chubby baby Frankie," I coo. "Did you miss Mama?"

Frankie flips over and yelps, immediately wanting belly scratches.

Frankie was my dad's beloved short-haired, red classic dachshund. He might have been originally my mother's, but it soon became apparent who he favored. And that'll happen when you feed a wiener dog a ton of scraps and snacks right from the table and recliner every night.

Frankie's coming up on nine years old, and being overweight—well, morbidly obese according to the vet—he's become diabetic, and needs daily insulin shots alongside a diet he *hates*. Which is probably why I've caught him on the counter eating bread and cookies several times.

I still have no idea how he gets up there.

Unhooking him from his line, I let him inside with me. We go through our nightly routine of dinner, walkies, shower, and snuggles. I sigh heavily as I sit on the couch with Frankie's fat booty plopped in my lap. "What do you think, Frankie, should I go out for margaritas tonight?"

Frankie looks up at me with a huff, going back to the old westerns on TV he used to watch with my father on Saturday nights. I swear he knows when it's a Saturday. If you don't put it on for him, he cries and cries until you do.

He really is a big baby.

Reluctantly—and for the first time in easily a year—I decide I should. I mean, there *is* a special on margaritas. If anything, the bar will be filled with ladies, right?

Right.

Grabbing Frankie's couch blanket, I wrap him up and put him in his favorite spot. I turn the TV volume down some and leave it on for him while I'm out. I change quickly into—what used to be—my find-a-man dress. It's currently all I have that's cute and not in the wash. Slipping into the simple, black cocktail dress with skinny straps. It cuts off just below my ass and sinches to my waist just right.

It's always been my go-to when I'm looking for a quick night with a quick fella.

But not tonight.

Tonight, I'm just hoping to let loose and have a few drinks.

Shaking my hair out into neater waves, I slap on a full face of makeup with hot red lips. I grab my leather jacket, stuffing a few cards and cash in the inner pockets with my phone. I slip into my favorite red pumps, and I'm out the door.

But not before giving Frankie a big smooch. "I'll be home in a few hours. Be good, and you stay off the counter, mister. I love you," I scold him with love before I close and lock the door.

My Uber pulls up, and before I know it, I'm outside a jam-packed Tavern Nine. Tipping the driver, I slide out and saunter to the front door. The bouncer studies me, up and down with a grin and—not even bothering to check my ID—lets me in.

The band is already playing their set as I make a beeline straight to the bar where Garrett's waving me over while simultaneously pointing to the far corner. I turn. *Crap.*

Madison and Colt are here.

I'm going to need a few strong drinks in me if I'm going to stick around here tonight.

Four.

Butch

THE BAND STARTS THEIR set, and the whole night takes off.

It's early, not even after nine, but I'm about ready to go. I'm tired, and I've already been asked to fuck in the bathroom by a *very* horny cougar—who had to be in her fifties with a big ass margarita in hand.

"I can't believe that chick asked if she could *climb you like a tree*, Butch." Tanner shakes his head, still in shock.

Stan nudges his arm. "Kid, that was no *chick*, that was a *woman*. A prime cougar in her natural habitat looking for a log to perch on." He laughs at his shit joke, clinking glasses with Tanner as they down their shots.

I scan the bar, not seeing anything worthwhile. Which is saying a lot since the place is packed shoulder to shoulder full of people. But

I do catch sight of Garrett Clark and a few of his buddies sitting at the bar.

And I'd be lying if I said I didn't have an itch for a fight tonight.

Reading my thoughts, Stan snorts. "Reel it in, Butch. You're not winning any points beating the shit out of Garrett Clark."

"Points with who?" Tanner asks quickly, and too curiously for my liking.

I snarl, "None of your fuckin' business."

Stan chuckles darkly. "Someone's in a mood tonight."

"He's always in a fuckin' mood." Duke, my younger brother, laughs heartily, slapping me on the shoulder. "How the hell are ya, bro?"

"Fine," I grunt, taking a swig of my beer.

Duke is only a year younger than me, but we might as well be twins with how alike we appear at first glance. He owns and operates a mechanic shop right in the center of town. About the only difference between us might be our personalities at this point—aside from my beard and his short scruff.

There are five of us Montgomery sons. In running order; myself, at thirty-four, I own *Montgomery Logging*. Duke at thirty-three, owning *Montgomery Repair & Towing*. Beau at thirty-two, with a few vacation rental cabins running while he's enlisted in the Army, currently stationed overseas. Rhett at thirty and Levi at twenty-eight, both owning *Montgomery Construction & Lumber* that they operate together.

We've got a sister, Lily, who's the youngest at twenty-five. Lily's got a son, my nephew, Parker. He just turned three when she moved back home with our parents so they can help her raise him. Parker's father, Chet, left for an oil job in Texas. That was over a year ago, and no one's heard from dead-beat-Chet since.

It also doesn't surprise me one bit that Lily's here with a large group of her friends, dancing and watching the band play. When she should be home with her son, considering she was just here last night.

"You scoped out any ass for the night?" Duke chuckles, swigging his beer in hand.

My jaw tightens. I might settle for busting my brother's nose over Garrett's tonight. A welcome change, if I do say so. Before I can rattle off some fighting words, Stan backhands me in the chest. "Holy shit—look who just walked in."

I glance over to the front door, scanning the crowd. That's when I see her—a ray of sunshine beaming through a dark cloud. *Cassidy's here.* And like the seas parting to let me get a better look at her, the crowd shifts, giving me a clear view of her for a good moment.

And, *fuck*, she is stunning tonight.

I feel it in my cock as I take in the sight of her from head to toe. She does a quick survey around the bar. For a second, I worry she might be here for a date, but when she starts making her way over to Garrett, I breathe a sigh of relief.

"This might be your shot, man," Stan tells me. "It's two-for-one margaritas. Ya gotta know that's why she's here."

"Wait." Duke's brow furrows, gesturing to Cassidy leaning over the bar with her perfect ass popped out talking to the bartender. "You got the hots for Cassidy Clark? Don't you beat the shit out of her brother all the time?"

There goes that vault kept secret.

Tanner starts to snicker. I shoot him a glare with a low growl in warning that shuts his ass right up. "No," I say. "I don't beat the shit out of him *all the time.* Just when he wants to start shit."

Stan laughs.

Duke grins. "Damn, Butch, I didn't know you could have a crush anymore. Thought you planned to die alone on that mountain."

"She wrote *Smile, Asshole* on his cup yesterday," Stan blurts out to Duke like he's been holding that in for more than a damn day. "Even put a little heart over the 'I' for him."

Duke chuckles, dragging over a seat. "Yeah, this could be a good use of my Saturday night." Looking back over to where our sister is dancing with her friends, he adds, "Why don't you ask if Lily can hook y'all up? They used to hang out in high school. I mean, it's been a while, but I'm sure she could work some magic for ya."

"No," I deadpan. Knowing damn well the second Lily hears about this, the whole goddamn town is going to know. Which means Cassidy will know, and I'm not going to find another place to get my morning coffee on the way to work. Hell, I started going there for her to begin with.

Now, I love the coffee, food, and the sight of her each morning to start my day.

"Come on, Butch. This is probably the first time you've seen her outside the coffee shop in...how long? You've got to make a move," Stan points out.

He's not entirely wrong. I'm thinking the same thing.

Duke nods. "Stan's right, bro." Glancing over to Cassidy downing a shot of tequila with her brother and laughing while he hands her one of two strawberry margaritas on the bar. "And if you don't, I might just have to say hello myself."

A growl works its way out of my throat before I can think otherwise. I lunge forward, pushing my chair back with a loud scrape and grab him by the collar of his shirt. "You try and I'll knock your fuckin' teeth out."

Duke booms with laughter, holding his hands up in surrender. "I said, I'd go say *hello*. I didn't say I'd try anything. You're callin' dibs, I get it."

I shove my hold off him, sitting back down at the pub table we got along the wall with a grunt. *He's just messing with me*, I tell myself. Duke's not even looking for anything.

Fuck. I'm sitting here acting like she's already mine when she's not.

Not *yet*.

"All right, so what's the plan?" Stan asks with a little *too* much excitement, yet again. "We can wait it out a bit, make sure she's got a few drinks in her first."

"Yeah, but then some other prick might swoop in," Tanner says, nodding to the bar. "Like this dipshit now."

We all turn to watch some guy I don't recognize walk over to Cassidy. A tourist, maybe? He leans over, smiles, and whispers something in her ear while placing a hand on her lower back. My jaw clenches at the sight, and my hold on my beer tightens. Cassidy jerks back, shaking her head and saying something to the guy. He nods and walks away.

Cassidy rolls her beautiful eyes and chugs her margarita, grabbing her second.

"Well, damn, that was a fast shutdown," Stan says, and I cringe. It was.

I don't think I've ever been shot down like that before. What the hell would I do if she did that to me? Three years I've told myself I need to get my shot in with this chick. For three *years* I've wanted her.

I...can't imagine never having a chance to make her mine.

Duke shifts his seat until we all kind of angle our stools to watch the bar where Cassidy is. "I say wait until she's had at least three," my brother states.

"Nah, she's already had two shots and one margarita," Stan counters. "She'll be spent after two with how strong the bartender is making those tonight. Did you see the amount of tequila he was pouring in that blender?"

"She might have a high tolerance," Tanner reasons. "Garrett can drink like no fucker I've ever met."

"True," Duke agrees.

I don't say a word. What am I supposed to say? I'm still trying to figure out what the hell I'd even say *to* her if I get the opportunity tonight.

The four of us sit and watch.

We watch Cassidy laugh and chat with Garrett and his friends. A few of her girlfriends show up and yank her around for hugs. They take shots together until most of them disperse with guys or to dance. But not Cassidy, she's been hit on four times now, by four different men. Each time she smiles kindly with a firm *"No, thank you."* and goes straight back to her margarita.

It's nearing eleven, and she's downed three shots, a double, and is somehow working on her third margarita. This is about when I start to notice her sway a little. Her cheeks flush and she's taken off her jacket, exposing her lightly tanned shoulders beneath her hair cascading down to her mid-back.

Garrett's got some girl on his lap, sucking her face dry. The band starts to play a rock-like tune and Cassidy starts to sway her body to the music. She leans over the bar, saying something to the bartender. He nods as she hands her jacket over the bar, putting it under for her.

She picks up her margarita and moves over to the dance floor. Garrett and the chick follow with their drinks in hand. They start to grind while Cassidy dances alone. Rolling her body slowly, as if she's feeling every beat from the band.

I wonder for a second if this is my shot.

"Now's your chance," Stan says, shoving me hard in the shoulder. "Get in there."

I hesitate, unsure of myself for the first time in my life. "She's had too much."

Duke scoffs. "Isn't that the point of us sitting here for the last two hours watching her drink? Quit being such a pussy and get the hell over there."

They're right. It's now or never.

I down the remaining half of my beer and stand. As I start to make my way over, I catch sight of yet another prick swaggering over to her and resting a hand on her waist. *Shit.* I wait a beat, watching, but when Cassidy finally focuses on the guy...she shoves him away.

Being just within earshot, I hear her say, "Get away from me, Colt."

It's then I realize who he is. Colt Lewis. Another local I can't stand, and one I'd love to beat the hell out of, actually. He doesn't seem to get the message to *fuck off*, either. He reaches out, roughly grabbing Cassidy's arm to the point she spills her drink on him. There's fear in her eyes, plain as day. And rage in his as she tries to violently pull away from him.

"Let me go. Please," Cassidy cries out.

I move.

Pushing through the crowd to get to her, Garrett attempts to grab Colt, but he shoves him back, causing Garrett to fall into the girl he was dancing with. I fight my way to get around a group of people dancing, watching Colt drag Cassidy to the front door with him.

All I see is red as she starts to cry while desperately trying to break free from his hold. He starts dragging her through the crowd and straight to *me*. Perfect.

The moment he's within arm's reach, I grab him by his neck so tight he releases Cassidy instantly. She stumbles a little, and I catch her by the waist with my other arm, pulling her into me. Having her pressed against me feels...right. I find myself fighting the urge to draw her even closer, to feel as much of her body connected to mine as I can.

It takes her a second to get her footing before she glances up at me with wide eyes filled with tears. I've never seen her cry before. And the sight doesn't sit right with me. My chest tightens as she gazes at me like a sad, lost doe.

I'd do anything to never see another tear fall from those eyes, I realize.

I'm so fucked.

"What the *fuck*," Colt spits in my direction, throwing a punch that a toddler could dodge.

Releasing Cassidy, I start to drag this worthless motherfucker through the parting crowd and out the front door. Looks like I'm about to get that fight I was itching for.

Five.

Cassidy

"CASS," GARRETT SLURS, COMING to stand beside me as I watch Colt get dragged through the crowd and out the front door, by none other than Butch Montgomery. Three men follow them out. While several other people follow suit, no doubt wanting to see a fight. "Shit, Cass, you okay?"

I don't bother responding, because I am *not* okay.

I'm drunk as a skunk and not okay one bit.

Pushing my spilled drink into some random girl's hand, I make a beeline for the front door. Once I'm in the parking lot, I catch sight of Butch tossing Colt on the pavement with a heavy thud.

"Fight, fight, fight," chants some idiot in the smoking crowd. The bouncer starts pushing his way through the crowd to end this before it begins, but he's stopped by Duke Montgomery—who might as well be Butch's twin tonight. As he talks to the guy, Duke glances at me, his mouth lifting in a smug smirk.

My brow furrows. *Am I missing something here?*

Meanwhile, Colt gets to his feet. "Mind your own fuckin' business, Montgomery."

"How 'bout you show me what you're made of, tough guy," Butch growls.

I subconsciously take a step forward. I don't know why I do; I just do.

And I instantly regret it.

Colt sees me and his lip curls in disgust. "What is this shit, Cassidy? You with this asshole now? I always knew you were a tramp—"

Butch doesn't let him say another word. He reels back with his massive fist and punches Colt square in the face. I gasp as Colt lands hard on the ground with a thud. He's spitting blood as he tries to haul himself up with a dazed look in his blackening eye.

Part of me shivers with pure delight at the sight of Butch defending me. Protecting *me*. While another part, the foggy confused part of me, doesn't understand what or why it's even happening.

Colt laughs darkly. "She's a good fuck. I get it, man."

I don't even have time to be offended by my ex's disgusting comment before Butch is grabbing him by the collar of his shirt and hauling him to his feet. When he draws him in, Colt tries to throw a fist at him, adding a kick or two. But Butch doesn't let him get a single shot in, landing a hard uppercut to Colt's gut. He doubles over and Butch knocks him hard again, right in the jaw with his brutal fist.

The sheer force of it throws Colt back down in a heap on the cold pavement.

My hand slaps over my mouth as I start to cry—Why? I'm not entirely sure of that myself. Confused, I hurry back inside for my coat and to get the heck out of here. "Cass, Cass, slow down. Where you goin'? The night's still early," Garrett slurs with a smug grin. He smacks Mindy's ass, making her giggle. "Right, baby?"

Ignoring him, I get my jacket from the bartender and throw him a twenty. I tug on my coat and take my phone out, stumbling to the door as I attempt to order an Uber through my glossy drunk, tear-filled eyes. *Jeez, this phone screen is bright.*

Pushing out the front door, I stumble and sway, stopping off to the side to kick off my heels—since they *clearly* don't seem to be doing me any good. I reach for them just as someone comes up beside me. I jolt up so fast I see stars. Swaying, I start to fall back when a strong arm catches me.

"You called it, Butch. She's had way too much."

I narrow my eyes at the look-a-like Butch standing off to the side. His brother, Duke, I remember. "Buzz off," I snap. Following the strong, tatted arm wrapped around my waist to the face of the town asshole himself. He caught me.

I stare up at him for a long moment. His dark eyes are seemingly softer, yet still full of...something else, I can't quite figure out.

Pushing out of his hold, I fix my dress. "Thanks."

"Do you need a ride?" Butch asks me.

I shake my head *way* too quickly with a combo sway on my loose feet. "No, I got a car coming." I check my phone to see the ride time saying twenty minutes out. "Shit."

"Come on, I'll take you home," Butch says, reaching out to take my arm. I pull back before he can touch me—again, I note.

"Don't touch me," I scold. Leaning against the building I've somehow ended up beside, I put my head in my hands. Not even realizing I've started to cry until I find myself sniffling, "I should've left when I saw him here."

"What did you do, Cassidy?"

I lift my head to Madison storming over to me while Colt's busy getting picked up off the ground by the bouncer, holding his bloodied, beaten face.

Good. The low-life jerk.

Pointing her manicured finger in my face, she screams, "You think you can just get someone to beat up Colt because you're jealous. You're such a *bitch*!" I flinch back at her words. "Colt told me *everything*. You lied about him hitting you, all because you didn't want us to be together. You're a liar and a—"

"That's enough." With a tower of muscle and a low growl in his throat, Butch forces his way between Madison and me.

"You think I'd lie about something like that, Maddy?" I cry. "Screw you. And him. When he does the same to you, maybe then you'll believe me." The moment the words leave my mouth,

I know I don't mean them. I'd never want to see Madison hurt. Ever.

We might not be on good terms, but I know in my heart, I'd still be there for her if she needed me. She was my best friend for eighteen years. We grew up together.

Hot, fresh tears stir up behind my glossy gaze.

"You're such a liar," Madison shouts with a frustrated scream and stomp of her heel.

The sight has me laughing despite myself. And since I've had a few too many, I say the things I don't mean just to hurt her the way she hurt me. "Both of you can go to hell for all I care. Ride his little dick on the way down." I push off the wall outside the bar and walk away with my heels in hand. Hopefully, appearing more confident than I feel.

"Fuck you, whore," Colt shouts.

I chance a glance back over my shoulder. Only to see Duke Montgomery getting in Colt's face alongside Tanner Wright and Stanley Hall.

What the hell is going on tonight?

"You better watch your fuckin' mouth, boy," Duke threatens, pushing Colt back with a bump of his broad, intimidating chest.

Madison tries to come after me, but the bouncer grabs her. The sight has me pausing, hurt washing over me in a tidal wave of emotions. Would she really try to hit me—to fight *me*? After everything?

Look-a-like-Butch gestures to real-Butch, tipping his head in the direction I'm heading. As if to tell him to follow me. And for some reason, he does. I don't even know the Montgomerys like that. I fill their orders at Cup O' Joe and hear a few things here and there on the town gossip line, that's it.

A massive shadow falls over mine under the dim glow of the parking lot lights. Turning around, I glare up. "Go. Away."

"You're drunk," Butch huffs. "Let me take you home."

I snort. "You're right, I *am* drunk. And I'm *this* close—" I pause to make a tiny gesture with my fingers, "—to completely losing my shit. So, for the sake of yourself and your apparent twin. Leave. Me. Alone."

"No."

I shake my head, turning away from him with a sarcastic laugh bubbling out of me. "Why don't you go throw away someone else's disposable cup art." I spin around to face him, all laughing ceased. "Why are you such an asshole anyway? That cup had two flowers on it. Two. And you had a damn cow over it. It. Was. A. Flower. It wasn't gonna hurt your dickhead reputation any."

Butch cocks a half grin, crossing his oversized—annoyingly sexy—tatted arms over his—annoyingly delicious looking—broad chest. I scoff, regarding him up and down to show my disinterest. Even though my drunken lady bits seem to be forgetting the dislike we have for this brute.

"I wish I had a fancy floral cup to throw in your face right now," I sneer. "You're such an ass, you know that? Of course, you do. You probably *love* to just crawl under people's skin and ruin their day. I bet that's why you keep coming in every morning, just to piss me off."

He waits a few beats, before his obnoxious presence asks, "You done?"

"No. I'm not," I bite out, gesturing to the bar behind him. "I didn't ask you to help me in there. I could've—" I stop myself short. Knowing in my current state, I couldn't have done much to stop Colt from dragging me around. Heck, I was trying and it wasn't doing squat. "Never mind," I say quietly, turning away from him as the tears start to fall yet again.

Ugh. I hate crying like this.

His warm presence comes up behind me. "Let me take you home, Cassidy."

I cross my arms over my chest, sniffling and watching down the street for this stupid white Ford to pick me up.

"Cassidy," he grunts, sounding rather impatient. "You do realize you never confirmed your Uber."

I freeze, trying and failing to remember if I did or not. *No, I did. Did I?* He's messing with me...right? Slowly taking out my phone, I look and...he's right. I didn't. And now the car is over thirty minutes away.

Could this night get any worse?

I should be snuggled up in bed with my fat sausage dog. Not drunk crying in the local bar parking lot. Putting my head in my hands, I crouch down on the ground and sob.

"You got this over here, bro?"

"Yeah, we're good. I'll see you tomorrow at Ma's," Butch says. I hear heavy steps walk off, while a mass of muscle and man comes down beside me. "Cassidy, I'm going to give you one more chance to get in my truck so I can take you home before I put you there myself."

I scoff sarcastically. "Yeah, okay."

"Have it your way."

Before I know what's happening, he's got me by my waist, throwing me over his hulking shoulder like the caveman he is. "Butch," I squeak in shock, reaching back and attempting to pull my dress over my ass. "Butch. Put me down."

He doesn't. Stalking off to the far end of the parking lot and over to his truck with me hauled over his shoulder.

"Put me down," I grit, my cheeks heating. "My ass is out."

To add insult to injury, he laughs. "Guess you should've thought of that before you put this dress on."

I roll my eyes. "Oh, yeah, because when I picked this outfit, my first thought was; I hope some jerk throws me over his shoulder and carries me across the parking lot so my whole ass is out. Showing every Tom, Dick, and Harry the goods."

We reach his truck a second later and he hits the unlock button. He opens the passenger side door and sets me gently on the front seat. I quickly yank my dress down, already knowing he's seen my black seamless thong.

"You're not taking me home," I say in complete drunken defiance. "I'll wait right here for my ride."

His nostrils flare, scowling that signature scowl directed solely at me. "Sure, Cassidy. Whatever you say." He closes the door and loops around to the driver's side. When he gets in, he looks over at me with a raised brow. "So, how long are we waiting for your ride to get here? Since I'm sure you confirmed it by now."

Embarrassment wages a war in my mind with stubborn defiance. I suck in a lungful of air at the same time I cover my face to hide a wracking sob.

Stupid Uber. Stupid bar. Stupid two-for-one margaritas.

Butch sighs and starts his truck. "You live in Whitetail Park, right?"

Giving in, I nod weakly. "Yeah."

He pulls out of the parking lot and down the street to take me home. It's a quick seven-minute ride in silence to the park. I tell Butch which few turns to take to get to my trailer before he's stopping right out front and throwing the truck in park.

"Do you need me to walk you up?"

"I'm not a liar," I blurt out.

Wow, I really can't help myself tonight, can I?

Butch watches me for a long moment. "I know you're not."

I roughly wipe the rogue tear that escapes me, reaching for the door. "Thanks for the ride."

"I'm sorry about the cup," he starts, and I turn to him. "I wasn't trying to be a dick about it that morning. I had just gotten a call my grandmother died the night before, it wasn't anything personal against you, just bad timing."

I suck in a breath. Six months of regret hit me instantly. "I'm sorry. I...didn't know."

"Yeah, well, either way, I shouldn't have taken it out on you."

I nod slowly, not knowing what to say besides feeling like a complete *bitch* for holding a grudge over a silly cup the last six months when he'd just found out his grandma died the night before.

I'm the worst.

I push the door open fully and slide out with my heels and phone in hand.

"Do me a favor and flick your porch light a few times when you get in to let me know you're good," he tells me, running a hand down his face.

I hold the door open, looking at him with a mixture of confusion and...something else churning low in my belly. Tequila, maybe?

Not having the words, I simply nod and close the door. Making my slow, slightly swaying way up the porch steps, I push inside. Closing and locking the door behind me, I reach over and flick my porch light a few times like he asked. A moment later, I hear the rumble of Butch's truck pulling away.

I drop my shoes by the door and spin to gape at the couch where Frankie hasn't moved a single chubby muscle.

"Frankie, you won't *believe* the night I just had."

⁓

On the edge of their seats, Alison, Janice, and Peggy stare at me with wide eyes, listening to my fuzzy rendition of Saturday night. Janice isn't even scheduled this morning, but she overheard about the drama and made a point to be here to hear it firsthand.

By the time I'm done, they're silent until Alison blurts out, "That is *so* hot."

I laugh. "What is?"

"Um, *hello*. He beat the hell out of your scumbag ex for putting his hands on you in public," she says as if it's obvious. "That's just so..."

"Hot," Janice chimes in.

"Yes." Alison smiles. "Seriously, I would *die* to have a man defend my honor like that. How'd you not jump his bones right then and there?"

"Probably because I drank too much and was having a hard time even properly ordering an Uber." Which is true, but even as I say it, I wish I would've thanked him more than just for making sure I got home safe.

Peggy holds a hand to her heart, her eyes suspiciously glossy. "Did I ever tell you girls about the time Joe went to jail for beating my daddy close to death over fifty years ago?"

All of us gape at her at once.

Peggy sighs. "Well, Daddy was a drinker, the worst kind. He'd hit Momma and toss my sister and I around like we were rag dolls.

We'd hide, run, and even tried to lock him out of the house a few times. Well, one night, after a long stint on the bottle, he came home around the same time Joe was bringing me home from our first date. As you can guess, it didn't go so well. Daddy slapped me across the face right in front of Joe. I'd never seen such anger in Joe's eyes. Not even after that night. He beat my daddy to a pulp. He went to jail for a week before Momma and I went to the judge to defend him. We were married three weeks later and he never left my side for fifty-three years."

Janice takes Peggy's hand as she starts to sniffle. "He was a great man, Peggy."

"I hope you're not telling me I'm going to be married to Butch Montgomery in three weeks." I smile weakly, trying to lift her spirits. But on the inside, I'm a mixture of emotions. Can I even say that I know anything about who Butch really is? I can't say I do. I mean, small-town gossip only runs so deep. We all know most stories don't ever tell the full truth.

And I certainly can't hold my flower cup grudge against him a moment longer.

Peggy laughs, taking the tissue Alison hands her. "Maybe not three weeks. You can always wait four."

Janice chuckles.

Alison beams, glancing over to the clock. "You've got ten minutes to figure out what you're writing on his order, Cass. And it better be a good one considering you've been holding a grudge against the guy for a darn cup when he had just found out his grandma died."

Janice nods. "His grandmother's name was Rose. It probably didn't help it was roses on the cup either."

I groan. "I already feel like crap about it." Throwing my hands in the air. "What am I supposed to say now? I wrote *Smile, Asshole* on his last cup, granted he didn't mention it, but still. He had to of seen it."

"Maybe he didn't," Alison counters. "Either way, you need to say thank you a hundred times over, because that night could've ended so much worse if Butch wasn't there. You said it yourself, Colt had that look in his eye. He was going to hurt you, Cass."

I take in a deep breath, failing to reel it in on this one. "I know." I don't need them all telling me how grateful I should be for what Butch did for me—I already am. I haven't stopped thinking about it. Or him...

I might not have been the most cooperative the other night, but he didn't leave me when I needed someone the most. But this is *Butch* we're talking about. Butch 'The Town Asshole' Montgomery. What am I even supposed to do with that?

The same man every woman wants...except me.

Because I can't stand him...right?

"At least be friendlier toward the man," Janice says.

Peggy nods in agreement. "At the very least."

Alison nudges me suggestively with her elbow. "Extra-large, *extra*-friendly. If you know what I mean?"

Peggy and Janice laugh.

A few customers trail in, stopping the conversation short. I fill their orders on autopilot, my mind somewhere else entirely. The moment they're gone, I glance up just in time to see Butch's truck pull up. *Crap.* I grab his to-go cup and a Sharpie. Thinking fast, I write the only thing I seem to be able to come up with.

Why am I so nervous right now? I despised this guy two days ago.

The bell chimes as I start filling the cup with black coffee. Turning with his coffee in hand, I set it down on the counter in front of him with the short message facing me so he doesn't see it right away.

"Extra-large black coffee, two breakfast sandwiches, and a peanut butter cookie. To go," he grumbles, tossing a few bills on the counter. But instead of him staring at his phone like usual, he locks his eyes with mine. Deep brown irises bore into me with a scorching intensity. His expression, unreadable.

My breath catches in my throat.

I gather his order in a paper bag, pushing it over toward him while taking the money he tossed down. Butch makes a noise in his throat, grabbing his coffee and order.

Just as he turns to go, I say, "Have a good day."

My words seem to catch him off guard. *Was he waiting for me to say something?* He pauses, glancing back over his shoulder at me. "You, too," he grunts, stalking off toward the front door and out to his truck.

I blow out a long, exaggerated breath.

"Smooth." Alison giggles.

I glare at her as the three of them laugh at my expense.

"What did you write on his cup?" Peggy finally asks.

I sigh heavily. "I wrote *Thank you, C.*"

Janice inclines her head thoughtfully. "That's a good start. Now, what are we writing on it tomorrow? Because you can't stop after this."

I groan, and they all smile.

What the hell have I done?

Six.

Butch

I'M SMILING LIKE A fucking idiot right now, but it's only because I'm driving alone on my way to work. "*Have a good day,*" she said to me. I didn't expect her to say anything, honestly. I was expecting her usual Monday aggravated sigh, but instead, I got something better.

I shouldn't be this hyped, I really shouldn't. But when I pick my coffee back up from the cup holder of my truck, something catches my eye. Turning the cup, I read, "Thank you, C."

No shit. Another heart right there beside it, too.

My stomach does some weird flipping business that I'm not proud to admit. And I scowl at my reaction to two words, a shape, and a single letter written on a paper cup. Although, it is better than her calling me an asshole in fancy cursive.

Pulling up to the work site, Tanner and Stan race to my truck with grins on their faces like the idiots they are. I kill the engine and push open the door.

"What's it say?" Stan immediately questions.

I scoff. "Y'all are worse than a couple of teenage girls."

Tanner laughs.

Stan rolls his eyes. "Just show us the damn cup."

I grumble several curses under my breath and grab my coffee to show them what Cassidy wrote. Stan narrows his eyes to read, leaning back and smiling wide. "Well, hot damn, another heart."

"Nice," Tanner beams. "You're so in, boss."

I huff, stepping out of my truck. "I'm not *in*, Tanner. She wrote a thank you, that's it."

Stan claps. "Exactly. Now's your chance to say something more to her. Hell, wait until Friday, see what she writes throughout the week, and then ask her if she's doing anything this weekend. And let the magic flow from there."

"I like it," Tanner says, giving Stan a high-five.

I scowl. "How 'bout y'all quit dickin' around and get to work."

The two idiots laugh as they head over to start working the mountain with the others. Once they're out of sight, I look down at the cup in my hand with Cassidy's perfect handwritten thank you.

Would it be weird if I kept this cup?

What am I even thinking? Yeah, it would be.

As bad as I want her, I'm not a stalker. After the last six months of being on her shit list, I better play this out carefully, because I can't wait another three years to get my shot at being with her.

The rumors are already flying around town about us after Saturday night. The worst part about it is a few more of Colt's exes have chimed in on the drama. Claiming he is an abusive piece of shit, which has only fueled my rage toward him and what he could've possibly done to her that night if I wasn't there.

All the more reason why he'll be getting his ass beat down a few more times by yours truly.

By the time Friday came around, I bailed on asking Cassidy out since I knew I'd be working the boys overtime Friday and Saturday. It wasn't ideal, and I hate making them work weekends, but there was an order that needed filling that I couldn't pass up for the pay. So we worked.

It's been another whole week, and we're finally wrapping up on this Thursday right on time. Cassidy's been leaving me little messages on every cup for the last two weeks, and I think I've memorized every last one.

Monday: Thank you, C.

Tuesday: Enjoy a good morning with a Cup O' Joe.

Wednesday: Have a nice day!

Thursday: Don't sweat the small things.

Friday: Work hard until your good is better than your best.

Monday: Wake up & live your dream.

Tuesday: Don't worry, be happy.

Wednesday: Your best day is yet to come.

Thursday: When life gives you lemons, throw 'em!

I'd be lying if a few didn't make me grin from ear to ear.

I was surprised they weren't something frilly or lame, they're genuinely meaningful—to me? Which is weird, because before the whole flower cup incident, the quotes were pretty girly for my taste. Stan swears she's custom writing these for me. Even Duke chimed in on the conversation, saying there's no way she's not because the other day, his said; *Wake up and feel pretty.*

Could she really be thinking of *me* when she's writing these each morning? The thought alone is giving me a bit more confidence in this. Whatever *this* is. And what it could turn into.

Packing up for the day, Stan makes his way over. "So, is tomorrow going to be *the* day? Are we asking Cassidy Clark the breakthrough question?"

I scoff. "I don't think asking what she's got goin' for the weekend is a breakthrough question."

Stan crosses his arms over his chest. "Man, you're slow, aren't ya? I've read every cup, same as you. You can't give me that shit. She tells you good morning when you walk in, and have a good day when you leave. What more do you want? Because your caveman grunts of *you too* back to her are lamer than watching Tanner try to score."

I cock a half grin. "And watching you is any better?"

Stan scoffs, waving me off. "Whatever, you're a lost cause. I was hoping to play Uncle Stan someday, but I guess that's a damn pipe dream."

"I'll ask her," I grumble, tossing my hard hat in the back of the truck.

"You'll pussy out."

"I said I'd fuckin' ask her, I'll ask her."

Tanner comes over with that eavesdropper grin. "There's another live band this weekend at Tavern Nine. Jack told me they're doing the margarita special again. Said they made bank last time."

Stan snorts. "I bet they did."

"You really think after last time she'll want to go there of all places?" I ask. "Because I highly doubt it."

Tanner shrugs. "She was having a good time from what I saw before that asshole showed up. No doubt she'd be down for a good time to make up for that bullshit."

Stan slaps Tanner on the shoulder like a proud father. "Not bad, kid." Turning to me, he says, "You got your line, work on it tonight. Don't go fuckin' stuttering or some shit. I know this is your first time on the other end of things."

Tanner's mouth hangs open. "*What?* He's never had to hit on a chick before? What the—I need to start working out."

I tug Tanner into my side, throwing a heavy arm over his stocky shoulders. "Stick with us kid, and we'll get the ladies workin' for you."

Stan guffaws. "Yeah, until you find one you obsess over for three years, but don't have the balls to talk to."

I scowl, punching Stan in the arm as hard as I can. He winces and grabs his arm. "Fuck you, Butch. Ya know what, I hope she tells you to go suck your own dick."

Tanner gives me a thumbs up. "I'm rootin' for ya, boss."

I slap Tanner hard on the back. He winces. "No one likes a kiss ass, Tanner."

~

I slept like shit last night. Which never bodes well for my mood. Not that much does, but still. Waking up this Friday being the day I'm going to make a *move* on Cassidy...well, it's not the day to be a top-notch prick.

I pull out of the long drive on my ten acres where my solid two-story, three-bedroom, two-bathroom log cabin sits with views for days and an overhang porch I nearly died building. Equipped with a boner-inducing mancave in the basement and a separate two-car garage that Duke envies. The fact I live here alone is heaven, most days. And other days hell.

I'll never admit it to anyone, but it gets lonely being the town asshole.

Maybe I should get a dog?

I make the fifteen-minute drive over to Cup O' Joe in no time at all. My leg is jumping, I'm tapping the steering wheel like a nervous dweeb. What the hell is wrong with me? All I'm asking is if she's doing anything this weekend, and going from there. But *where* am I going from there? What do I say after that?

Shit.

"Be cool," I tell myself, parking out front of the coffee shop. "Don't be an asshole."

With the pep talk of the century ringing in my ears, I hop out of my truck and make my way inside. The bell chimes and Cassidy's already filling up my coffee like always. Approaching the counter, she sets the cup down in front of me. "Morning," I say.

She smiles up at me. A smile so stunning my face heats. *Be cool. Don't be an asshole*, I remind myself, *and stop blushing, you loser.*

"Morning," she replies, moving toward the display. "What kind of cookie will it be today?"

"Chocolate chunk will do." I toss a twenty on the counter to buy me some time while she gets my change for once.

She nods, getting my two breakfast sandwiches and cookie, putting them in a bag and placing them beside my coffee. When she takes the money and starts gathering my change, I know it's now or never. "You got any plans this weekend?" I ask, far more casually than I feel.

Cassidy hums, tipping her head to the side. "Catching up on laundry most likely." She bumps the register drawer closed with her hip as she hands me my change. "You?"

I toss the coined change in the tip jar, pushing the bills into my pocket. "They've got that live band playing tomorrow night at Tavern Nine again. You planning on going?"

Cassidy raises a brow at me. "Are you?"

"Yeah."

My cock throbs watching her draw her plump lower lip between her teeth. She watches me for a long moment—long enough that I'm about ready to throw myself into oncoming traffic if she doesn't say something soon.

"Maybe I'll see you there," she finally says with a small smile.

I fight back the twitch at the corner of my mouth. Keeping my expression impassive, I grab my coffee and breakfast. "Sounds good."

Cassidy's smile grows. "Have a good day."

I nod, turning and heading to the door. "You, too." When I get to my truck, I play it cool until I pull out and down the road before I grab my coffee. Turning it, I read, "One tequila, two tequila, three tequila, floor."

The smile that spreads across my face is painfully wide and genuine. I chuckle to myself, something I don't do often. And I don't think I've ever had a faster mood change than I just had in my fucking life.

I might actually have a shot at this.

Seven.

Cassidy

"Sooo, he asked you out...indirectly?" Alison questions.

"I mean, yeah, I guess so." I shrug. "All I said was maybe I'd see him there. I didn't say I'd go."

"But you're going, right?" Janice chimes in, cashing out a customer and taking the next in line.

It's a Saturday afternoon and I asked Alison to meet me here so I could talk to her about yesterday's odd encounter with, none other than, Butch Montgomery. And since I know for a *fact* he only comes in Monday through Friday, I knew it was a safe bet not to run into him here. Even on my days off I always end up coming in it seems.

I scrunch my nose. "I don't know. Last time didn't exactly pan out."

"But you said you were having a great time before that crap with Colt," Alison reminds me. "And if Butch is there, he's not going to let anything like that happen again. It's a win-win."

Janice agrees, "I'd go. You need to have fun once in a while, Cassidy. I mean, it's your day off and you're here for Pete's sake."

I sigh heavily. She's not wrong.

Alison sips her iced tea. "I'd love to go with you, but I'm working at the gas station tonight. I get out at midnight. If you need a ride home, let me know. It's on the way."

"Midnight?" I repeat. She nods. "I don't know if I want to stay out that late."

She laughs. "Oh, come on, Cassidy. What do you have going on? Going home to Frankie's fat ass and helping him get off the counter. By the way, have you figured out how he's been getting up there?"

I smile. "No, I haven't. I think he might be wearing a fat suit to fool me, or have leg extenders hidden somewhere." Janice and Alison laugh heartily. "Okay, fine. Pick me up at midnight like Cinderella, but instead of it being from a castle, it's from the bar."

"Make sure you text me if you end up going home with any *suitors*." Alison winks. I openly scoff, waving her off. "I can always pick you up from Butch's castle." She winks again lamely.

"Oh, yes," Janice beams. "Have you seen his house? It's breathtaking. I heard he built it himself with his brothers and father. It's as close to a castle as you'll get around here."

Warmth spreads through my chest. He built his house with his family? Why is that so...attractive? Wholesome? Not at all sounding like the asshole I've known and heard about for years.

"No, I haven't," I mutter under my breath, my mind jumping from one strange feeling to another.

"What are you going to wear?" Alison asks me. "Because I've seen your black mini-dress, and I'm not sure you'll be able to top that."

Janice hums. "True, you can't wear that again. What else do you have?"

"Oh." Alison bounces, full of giddiness over whatever revelation she just had. "I know. Those daisy dukes you wore that day we went hiking. Your ass was nearly falling out of those things."

I frown. "Yeah, and I got the worst chafe between my thighs *because* of those damn things."

"Well, you're not going hiking, and you need to show the *assets*, missy," Janice says. "That's how I scored Billy. He might be a heap now, but he was a hunk back in his hay day."

Alison and I share a laugh as Janice snickers. Janice may be only forty-five, but she talks like she's a mixture of twenty and sixty all at once.

"I did buy this new off-the-shoulder black blouse. It might look good with those shorts," I say.

"Yes." Alison claps. "Oh, and do me a favor, find out if Tanner is single."

I raise a brow. "Tanner Wright? Really?"

Blushing, Alison's lips purse. "What? He's cute."

I bite my lip, glancing at Janice who's shaking her head with a smile. "Isn't he like, freshly twenty-one?"

Alison huffs, giving me a side-eye. "No. His Facebook says he's twenty-three, thank you very much. And he's got a real job—I mean, he still lives with his parents, but he's living in the room above the garage, so it's kind of like an apartment."

I tip my head to the side. "I thought you liked them older, not a year younger than you."

"I thought you liked them a max of five years older than *you*, not ten years like Butch," she snaps back with some extra sass behind her.

I scoff loudly. "I never said I *liked* him. Besides, considering he could've been arrested for beating Colt for me, it's only fair I—I don't know...be friends with him? And ten years isn't bad."

"Ha." She points a finger right in my face. "I knew it!"

She really won't let this one go. "I didn't say anything." I wave her off. "You know what, forget picking me up."

Alison waves me off in return. "Quit being dramatic, I'll pick you up. But when Butch and you end up K-I-S-S-I-N-G in the parking lot, I'll be the one snapping pictures as proof to show around town."

"And to me," Janice adds with a laugh.

I shake my head, smiling despite myself.

I'm late.

But that's what happens when your diabetic dog eats half a package of defrosting hotdogs on the counter while you're in the shower. *Dammit, Frankie.* I really need to get a camera set up to see how the hell he does it.

It's almost 9:30 PM as I hurry to the front door of Tavern Nine, and the place is just as packed as last time, if not more. The bouncer eyes me with a smug grin, earning an eye roll from me.

I went with the ripped daisy dukes and off-the-shoulder black blouse. My makeup is better than I've done in months—I seriously have no idea how I got matching winged eyeliner on both sides. On my first try, mind you. I decided to ditch the heels in place of my flip-flops, in case I need to make a run for it again tonight.

Thankfully, it's late June and a beautiful night.

The bouncer gives me a dip of his head in acknowledgment, again not bothering to check my ID as I squeeze my way inside. I take a quick scan of the bar and note the unfortunate sight of my brother and his drinking buddies by the bar with Mindy on his lap yet again. I shake my head, weaving around a few people until I see a tall, tower of muscle I recognize with his back to me ordering from the bar.

He's got on dark wash jeans, a pair of black steel-toed boots, and a tight black T-shirt, making his thick muscled arms pop. He somehow appears bigger with his black and grey tattoos on full display.

I smile, going to him. "Hey."

Butch glances back over his shoulder and all the way down to me. His expression quickly morphs from one of annoyance to one of surprise. It's almost comical. "Hey."

"Sorry, I'm late. My dog got into some hotdogs," I tell him, leaning over the bar to get Jack, the bartender's, attention.

"No worries," he says, seeming to relax a little more at the sight of me. I inch closer to him to make room for others trying to squeeze in near the bar. "What are you drinkin' tonight?"

"Not sure yet." I point to his beer in hand. "Are you a strictly beer drinker?"

"Beer or whiskey."

"Hey, Cass, what'll it be?" Jack asks me. "We've got the margarita special going, but I'll tell ya, they're not as strong as last time. Apparently, I was overdoing it on the tequila." He chuckles.

That's an understatement.

I smile. "I think I'll pass on the margaritas tonight, Jack. Get me a shot of tequila and a Mexican mule."

"You got it," he slaps the counter, heading off to make my drink.

I reach into my purse to pull out my wallet, but Butch stops me with his heated, calloused hand on mine. "I got it," he says, tossing a fifty on the counter.

"Oh. Thanks."

"So, what's in a Mexican mule?" he asks.

"Ginger ale, tequila, and lime," I reply. "They're addicting if made right."

Jack comes back over with my shot and drink. He takes the cash and gives Butch his change. Holding my shot up to Butch's beer, I say, "Cheers."

He clinks my shot glass. "Cheers," he grunts, sounding reluctant to even say it out loud. I lick the rim of salt, swallow the shot down, and bite the lime. Butch swigs his beer, watching me with dark, avid eyes as I grab my drink and set down the empty shot glass and skin of lime. "We've got a table, if you want to come over."

"Sure."

He leads me through the crowd to the wall of high-top tables on the other side of the dance floor. When we get to the table, I'm greeted by the sight of Duke, Stan, and Tanner all staring at me with wide grins on their faces.

I hold back a cringe from how creepy they all appear right now with matching gleeful expressions. *Weird.*

Butch grabs a stool from a neighboring table and pulls it up for me. I hop up and get comfortable as he takes his seat next to mine. "I think you know my brother, Duke. That's Stan and Tanner."

Besides Duke being Butch's near twin, Stan's also pretty big. He's easily six-foot-one, with long dirty blonde hair pulled back into a low bun, lean with muscle, and a pretty boy face. Tanner's not bad-looking either, a little younger in appearance. He's maybe five-foot-eleven, stocky but built, with a few days' worth of patchy scruff on his face.

I give a little awkward wave to the table. "Hey."

Duke grins. "Nice to see you again, Cassidy. Hopefully, you won't tell me to buzz off tonight."

I smile, sipping my drink. "No promises."

Stan claps and stands from his stool. "Why don't I get us some shots? You do tequila right, Cassidy?" I barely open my mouth to confirm before Stan is heading back over to the bar.

"Did you have to work today?" Duke asks.

"No, I had the day off thankfully," I say. "I'm splitting a shift with Janice tomorrow, one of her older kids has a late soccer game."

Duke glances at Butch who clears his throat. "You said your dog got into something. Did he get sick?"

I wave him off with a laugh. "Oh, no, Frankie's fine. Just a half package of hotdogs gone. He's diabetic, so I had to watch him for a bit to make sure he was okay. The boy is a dumpster, I swear."

"What kind of dog is he?"

I smile at the thought of my favorite fat boy. "He's a red dachshund."

"You mean a wiener dog?" Tanner asks.

"Yeah, he was my dad's, so now he's mine."

"Right, I heard about old man Clark passing a while back," Duke says, his tone consoling. "I was sorry to hear. He was a good man."

I nod and sip my drink. "He was."

Butch looks like he's about to say something as a busty blonde comes sauntering straight over to the table. I think her name is...Lauren? I'm not sure. She's clearly had some work done, and she looks *damn* good in that tight red dress and cowgirl boots.

She leans over the table, her gaze solely on Butch as she licks her lips with a perky set of new boobs pushed out and inviting. "You ready for that dance yet, Butch?"

Duke scoffs. "Get lost, Lauren, he already said no. Quit being so desperate."

Lauren rolls her eyes, keeping her attention on Butch, who grunts a stern, "No."

She puts her hand on his arm, leaning in to whisper something in his ear. Butch scoffs loudly. He leans back and shakes off her hand. "Get fucked, Lauren."

She pouts. "That was the plan." Turning on her heels, she storms off.

"What'd she say?" Tanner asks eagerly the second she's out of earshot. And I'd be lying if I said I wasn't dying to know, too.

Butch glances at me, then back to Tanner. "Nothing."

"Come on, let's hear it," I tease, nudging him playfully with my elbow. "It was a blow job in the back, wasn't it?"

Butch raises a brow at me.

Duke booms with laughter while Tanner just stares wide-eyed in astonishment like he can't believe she could've offered him such a thing.

"I knew it."

"Seriously?" Tanner asks, shock written all over his face.

"Yup," I say, sipping my drink. "It's a wild world out there in the dating cesspool."

"She's Stan's ex, too," Duke grumbles. "That's why she waited until he walked away to come over. She did the same thing right before you got here."

I spit out my drink a little at that. Butch chuckles, handing me a napkin. "And she's over here trying to hook up with his friends right in front of him? Jeez."

Stan comes back a moment later with eight shots of whiskey and two shots of tequila for me. We all take a shot, clink, and drink.

This night might actually turn out to be a good one.

We're all rattling off jokes and talking shit about everyone and anyone around the bar. Telling stories and laughing so loud we're getting annoyed stares from the surrounding patrons. If you would've told me I'd be having this much fun with Butch Montgomery a few weeks ago, I would have told you to get checked into the looney bin. But right now, I am. We're all several drinks in, and I'm currently walking the line between buzzing to drunk.

"So, how come we've never seen you out until margarita night?" Stan asks me with a lingering chuckle.

I shrug, smiling. Heck, I think I've been smiling nonstop since I got here. "Men are assholes." I quickly wave a hand around the table. "No offense."

Duke groans, slapping Butch on the shoulder. "Aw, man, Cassidy. Don't tell me you're sworn off men right now?"

I roll my eyes. "No. I mean, it's hard to enjoy a night out when you're not looking for the attention, you know? Kind of like...when you're looking no one else is, then when you're not, they're everywhere, type of thing."

And just as I say that, Alex comes stumbling over to the table. "Ay, there you are, Cass. How the hell are ya?" he slurs, attempting to toss his arm around me, but I lean away, pressing my body into Butch's broad side.

Butch instantly takes the cue, shoving Alex's slimy outreached hand away.

Shock shows on the swaying nuisance. "Woah, man." He throws his hands up in surrender with a near-empty beer in hand. "Relax, we're cool. Cass and I go way back. Right, baby girl?"

I scrunch my nose, leaning further into Butch's side to get away from the stench of him. "Don't call me that, Alex. And go away, you smell like piss."

Alex scoffs, taking a step closer. "Don't be such a bitch, Cass."

A heavy, protective arm slides around my waist, drawing me in tighter. His masculine woodsy scent floods my senses and invades my space. I drink it in, inhaling long and deep as a heavy warmth envelops me.

Is it getting hot in here, or is it just me?

"She told you to fuck off. I'd listen if I were you because if she has to tell you again, I'll be doing it for her," Butch growls. And my lady bits swoon a little at the threatening undertone of his words.

Alex's drunken eyes widen, putting his hands up and backing away.

Once he's gone, I sigh, readjusting in my seat. "Thanks."

Much to my displeasure, Butch releases his hold on my waist. His hand caresses slowly over my back, warm and lingering as he pulls away. I fight the urge to lean back into him, to let him hold me like that again.

I bet he's a dream to curl up against on a cool night.

Huh. Where'd that thought come from?

Duke shakes his head. "Guess that's what you were talkin' about, huh?"

"Yeah." I sigh, downing the rest of my drink. The alcohol hits me instantly. And like the stars aligning, the band starts to play a song that just *screams* dance to me. Wiggling a little in my seat, I slip off to my feet. "Do any of you dance? Or are you a sit and watch kind of crowd?"

Duke raises a brow and I *swear* he kicks Butch under the table, but no one responds. I take off my purse and set it on the table. "You're all not gonna let me go by myself, are you?" I mock pout.

Stan groans dramatically, putting a hand to his back like he's faking an injury. "Ah, sorry, Cassidy, I messed my back up yesterday."

Tanner nods with a beaming smile. "Yeah, same here."

Stan shakes his head, laughing.

"I'm good," Duke tells me.

I turn to Butch, his lip curls in a mixture of a smile and a cringe. He invited me out tonight, I recall boldly. Not thinking twice, I grab his rough, mountain-worked hand. "Come dance with me." I bat my eyes and give his arm a gentle tug. "Please."

He groans, reluctantly standing—but I'm not sure how "reluctant" he really is because he's got a grin on his face that's saying otherwise. His hold on my hand tightens. "I can't dance for shit."

I giggle. "Neither can I. Come on." I tug him behind me onto the packed dance floor. The music booms a rock-country ballad with a hint of a grind to it, just the right amount you can roll your body to.

Butch grins down at me as I throw my arms up and around his thick neck. He leans down, gripping my hips with his strong hands as I start to sway and roll my body against his. He doesn't move much, just enough to make it look like he's not just standing there.

"Thanks for inviting me out," I say as he leans his head further down to hear me over the music.

His hands flex. Fingers curling into the belt loops of my shorts, he holds me tighter against him. "You havin' a good time?"

I nod, smiling up at him as my hand trails up the back of his neck threading through his hair. My nails gently scrape the back of his head in a light tease. Did I say I hated this guy a few weeks ago? Because that's starting to feel more like *decades* ago.

Butch growls, dipping his head toward my neck. His hot breath fans me, sending goosebumps over my already heated skin. "Me, too."

I can feel the heat building between us—and between my thighs. We dance like this for three more songs laughing, grinding, and teasing one another until he's telling Lauren to get lost again when she tries to cut in.

"Do you want another drink?" he finally asks, pulling away. I nod. "I'll get it. You head back to the table."

"Okay." I smile as he turns away, shamelessly gawking at his tight ass in those dark-wash jeans before he's swallowed up by the crowd.

When I take my seat back at the table, I realize how much I already miss that big mass of strong *man* pressed against me. I reach for my phone, catching Duke's cocky smile directed my way. Stan's busy with some girl on his lap, whispering in her ear, while Tanner watches them as if he's diligently studying whatever Stan's saying to make her laugh.

"Can't say I've ever seen Butch dance for four songs in a row like that," Duke comments.

Warmth flashes through me. "Oh, yeah?" I lean toward him over the table, trying to think of the best way to ask this. "What's his deal? I mean, I know he's had a good bit to drink like the rest of us, but he's actually being somewhat...nice? He's usually always such a dick."

Duke chuckles. "Yeah, I don't really know how to answer that honestly. It's just how he is." He shrugs. "He's not always an asshole. It's more like he saves the better side of himself for the people he cares about, ya know? The rest get, well, you know."

Oh, I do know. And I have to say, I'm liking this side of Butch a *whole* lot more. Maybe even a little *too* much, if I'm being honest with myself.

Tapping the side of my phone, I think for a beat if I should text Alison not to bother picking me up tonight. Should I? Truthfully, I'm not all that sure. Granted, I'm a tipsy sort of drunk, but I feel *good*. My head is clear enough. I'm having fun. And more so, I'm starting to enjoy the company of a certain broody mountain man.

Would it be wrong of me to want to extend the night a little further?

Before I can ask Duke what he thinks about the situation, a commotion steals everyone's attention. I follow the collective line of sight and watch my brother getting in Butch's face by the bar. Butch puts a hand on Garrett's chest, no doubt trying to keep him back, but Garrett's not letting up. He's shoving him back. *Hard*.

Can't I get one good night that ends well? Just *one*.

Standing from his seat, Duke sighs at the situation unfolding across the bar.

I grab my purse and stand, too, pushing through the crowd and over to Garrett trying to pick a fight, yet again. Butch is saying something to him, but whatever it is, my brother doesn't want to hear it. There's a fight wanting to be had in Garrett's eyes, glossed over with his misplaced rage.

I've seen that look before. He's in one of his drunken lows.

When I get within earshot, I catch my brother yell, "You think you're better than me, huh?"

Great. It's *this* low again.

I sigh heavily, coming up behind Butch at the same time Garrett shoves him, harder this time. Enough to push him into me. I yelp in surprise. Butch quickly wraps a strong arm around me, catching me before I tumble on my ass.

I don't even get a chance to catch my balance before I'm roughly yanked out of Butch's hold. "Get your fuckin' hands off my sister," Garrett booms.

Stumbling on my feet that can't seem to keep up with all the movement, I nearly topple over. Butch reaches for me, his jaw locked tight. He's holding back, I realize, for my sake. Pushing away from my brother, I move closer to Butch. "What the hell is your problem, Garrett?"

My brother's gaze darkens. "What's *my* problem? How about what's *your* problem, huh? You gonna sic your new dog after me, too? Just like you did with Colt and Alex."

Butch steps in front of me. "You're walkin' on thin ice, Clark."

"Take it outside," Jack shouts from behind the bar, pointing to the door. And for some stupid reason, they do. The crowd parts and I watch Butch and Garrett lock eyes, making their way to the door.

Crap. Rushing after them, Duke, Stan, and Tanner all follow. When we get to the parking lot, Garrett's immediately getting right in Butch's face.

Why does he have to do this now?

I push between them, shoving Garrett back with everything I have. "Back off, Garrett."

He takes a few steps back with my hands firmly on his abdomen, keeping his dark, drunk gaze locked behind me. "Did you fuck my sister, Montgomery?" Garrett demands, and I cringe.

Not only from his words but his tone. The disgust is right there on the surface.

"Better listen to your sister, Clark," Butch growls. "Wouldn't want you gettin' hurt."

Garrett tries to move me out of the way, but I shove him back harder. "You're such an asshole," I snap. Hot tears sting my eyes. Half for being utterly humiliated by my brother's current state, and the other half for having my night out with Butch ruined.

Suddenly, my arm is grabbed and I'm yanked away by Alex. The very second I'm out of the way, Garrett lunges for Butch. Stan and Tanner come over, prying Alex's hold from me while Duke stands off to the side with the bouncer, watching the whole thing. It's then, I notice, we've created quite the crowd outside the bar. All eyes facing this way.

This is worse than last time.

Butch seems to let Garrett get one good hit in. Only *one*. Because after that, it looks like all he sees is red. It's two hits to the face and one knuckle-cracking hit to the gut, and Garrett is on the ground in a pile.

Butch goes to take another step toward him—since apparently, he's not done. And that's when Duke finally steps in, putting a firm grip on his brother's shoulder, keeping him back from my very own brother on the ground. Bloody and curled into himself, he spits crimson over the gravel-ridden parking lot. A mixture of blood and snot pours from his nose.

"That all you got, pussy?" Garrett's bloody grin is like something a maniac would wear. I look over to Alex who's got a grimace on his face at the sight. Even *he* knows this is screwed up—and he's an idiot.

My brother starts to haul himself off the ground, wiping his bloody nose on his arm and spitting blood at Butch's feet. "All bark and no bite. What's the problem this time, Montgomery? Holding back because my *sister* is watching."

He throws another punch at Butch, who dodges it, shoving Garrett back instead. "That's enough, Clark."

Garrett stumbles back and I step forward, grabbing his arm before he falls. "Garrett, you're too drunk to—"

He shakes off my hold, sending his elbow right into my face. I yelp, jerking back. My hand cups my mouth as the taste of blood pools on my tongue.

Garrett spins around. "Shit, Cass, I—"

Butch lunges forward, yanking Garrett by the collar of his shirt and hauling him back. The bouncer seems to finally want to do his job, Duke and him attempting to break them apart.

"Cass, shit, are you okay?" Garrett tries to check on me, but Butch has lost his cool, shoving and throwing punches left and right. And that's about when they begin to brawl like animals.

I start to cry when I see Alison pull up. Grateful at the sight of her. Her eyes are wide, and she barely parks her car before she throws the door open and runs over to me. I quickly go to her, not looking back.

She tries to move my bloody hands to examine my mouth. "Oh my god, Cassidy. Are you okay?"

I shake my head, sobbing. "Let's just go."

Alison quickly ushers me to her car. We get in and she speeds off down the road, but not before I watch Butch throw one more hit right to Garrett's gut, making him throw up instantly.

Butch

Duke yanks me back just in time for me to watch Cassidy's friend Alison peel off down the road, taking Cassidy with her.

"You're fuckin' dead, Clark," I growl, trying to go after him again, but now I've got Duke, Stan, and Tanner, all holding me back. The thing is, they're not doing shit for the rage I have flaming inside of me right now over seeing Cassidy hurt.

Dan, the bouncer, has Garrett pinned up against the building as he hangs his head low with a mixture of blood, snot, and now vomit all over him. He's on the verge of tears as Alex takes hold of him at the same time the owner of the bar, Roger, comes storming out.

"Stand down, both of you," he shouts. "Or you'll both be banned."

My jaw is locked tight, grinding in time with the ticking bomb settled in my chest. I try to take in a deep breath, to reel my shit in. *Try*, being the key word. I shake off my brother and Stan and turn, heading to the dark end of the parking lot to cool down. They all follow. No doubt thinking I'm not done yet.

And I feel *far* from fucking done.

I rub my face roughly. "Fuck."

"What the hell happened back there, Butch?" Duke bites out.

I grit my teeth, turning back to look at Stan. "Was she okay?"

He runs a hand through his hair. "I don't know. I didn't get a look at it, but she had blood on her hands."

"I asked you a fuckin' question," my brother barks at me, shoving me hard in the shoulder to get my attention. As if I didn't hear him the first time. "What the *fuck* happened back there?"

"Prick was looking for a fight," I say. My jaw ticking, my fists flexing at my sides. "Same as he always is."

Tanner snorts. "Well, he got it all right."

"You don't go after him over a damn accident." Duke gets in my face. Venom and a harsh truth behind his words. "Garrett's a lot of things, but he didn't mean to hurt Cassidy. You want to release the beast, you do it on solid terms. That's how it works. And you'll be lucky if she ever speaks to you again after this shit."

I grind my teeth, turning away from him. He's right. I'll be lucky if she ever does speak to me again, let alone doesn't throw scalding coffee in my face come Monday morning. *Fuck*. Who am I kidding? I was lucky she even showed up tonight.

The whole night couldn't have gone better. I don't think I've ever had that good of a time with a woman over simple drinks and conversation. She's even more amazing than I had originally thought.

She's perfect.

And this is how the night ends.

"You better start using your head, bro. Cause if not, you *will* die alone on that fuckin' mountain," my brother threatens coldly, pulling out his phone. "I'm calling you a cab; you're done for the night."

I don't bother saying anything, there's nothing left to say. He's right. He always is. I fucked up. I should've gone to her, not after her goddamn brother. *I don't even know if she's okay.* And the thought alone is enough to have me drowning in guilt for the rest of my life.

There's no doubt in my mind, I just lost my only shot at Cassidy Clark.

The next morning comes agonizingly slow. I'm hungover and emotionally torn the hell up over last night. I haven't stopped thinking about it—about seeing her, making sure she's okay.

Which is currently where I'm heading. I remembered her saying she had to work the afternoon shift today at the coffee shop. So, against all my better judgment, I've decided to go to her house instead of her work. I don't want to make a scene in case she decides to tear me a new one.

Not that I'd blame her.

The plan is simple: ask if she's okay, apologize, and leave. No more, no less. Stan told me to bring her flowers or something, but after the flower cup drama, I didn't think that was as smooth of a move as he did.

Pulling up to her trailer, I park my truck beside her Jeep, kill the engine, and get out. Her place is tidy on the outside, with a few potted flowers here and there with a dog bed on the covered porch. There's a small shed pushed up against the rear of the trailer, but that's about it in the yard itself.

I blow out a rushed breath and thump up the porch steps. I wait a beat, suddenly second-guessing my plan. *No*, I tell myself, *I'm here*. She deserves an apology *now*. Not another six months from now. I bring my fist up, knocking on her door.

Don't be an asshole. *Don't be an asshole.*

Barks from what must be her dog are followed by a rushed, "One second," from Cassidy.

I take a step back, pushing my hands in my jeans pockets—a weak attempt at hiding the few cuts on my knuckles from last night. The door flies open, and I take in the sight of her. Her face is clean of makeup with a healing split bottom lip, and her hair is tossed up in a mess on top of her head. She's got on an old, oversized band T-shirt that goes well past her ass, and a pair of plaid pajama shorts.

But none of that is where my gaze lands, because she's got a wrench in her hand and there's water splattered all over her arms and shirt.

I open my mouth to start my spiel.

She points the wrench at me. "Do you know anything about hot water tanks?"

My brow furrows at the same time a fat wiener dog comes hobbling out the door and over to me with a wagging tail and a yip in greeting. "Yeah?"

Cassidy opens the door further. "If you help me, I'll accept whatever lame apology you've come to give me." Patting her leg, she coos, "Come on, Frankie, get back in here."

Frankie hobbles back into the house on command and Cassidy waves me in. I kick off my boots at the door as she closes it behind me. The place is clean, and fairly neat, but small. I'm barely clearing the ceiling. It's easy to tell what's new and what she's kept from her father.

I follow her through the kitchen area and down the narrow hall.

"I don't know what happened," she starts. "I just bought it not even three months ago. I followed all the instructions to put it in, and it's been working great. I was able to take a hot shower last night, but then this morning when I went to do the dishes, it's like ice."

I crouch down in front of the smallest closet known to man where the forty-gallon hot water tank sits and look it over. *How the hell did she get this in here by herself?*

"You installed this yourself?" I ask, trying to keep the disbelief out of my voice.

"Yeah," she says, bending down beside me. "Why? Did I do something wrong?"

Doing a quick run-through, she did everything right as far as I can tell. "Where's your fuse box?" I ask.

She opens the other side of the double-door closet, exposing the fuse box.

I nod, finding the problem right away. "The fuse to the water heater is blown. You'll need to get a replacement."

"Well, I got this at Andy's, do they have the replacement there?"

I stand. "They should. You'll need two for the kind you've got here."

"Okay." She sighs. "Thank you."

"I can, uh, do it for you if you want," I say. She glares up at me, crossing her arms under her breasts with a raised brow. I rub the back of my neck. "Listen, about last night..." I trail off, not remembering what I had rehearsed in my head.

Well, there goes that. *Nice job, asshole.*

Cassidy sighs, heavier this time. "Don't worry about it. I know it wasn't your fault. Garrett gets like that sometimes. He's usually a fun drunk, but he still dives head first into his lows every so often."

"Still," I press on. "It was a fucked-up way to end the night, and I'm sorry." My gaze trails over her stunning features only to land on her busted lip. "How's your lip?"

"It's okay. Just split. I iced it last night."

I nod, not knowing what else to say except, "Have you heard from your brother?"

She scoffs, gesturing back toward the kitchen. "Why do you think I woke up to a sink full of dishes? Wouldn't surprise me if he's the reason the fuse blew. Probably passed out in the shower again."

"Where is he now?"

"Heck if I know. Last night was probably the first night he's spent here in the last two months. He comes and goes as he pleases. Eats my food, makes a mess, drops off his dirty clothes, gets new ones, and leaves. It's a loving cycle we have going."

I scowl. "Sounds like it."

"Yeah." She bites her bottom lip for a second, wincing and releasing it quickly. "Anyway, I don't want to be rude, but I should probably get ready for work if I need to swing by the hardware store before they close."

"What time do you need to be at the coffee shop?" I ask.

"Eleven."

I got here at roughly 10:00 AM. "What time do you get out?"

A little wrinkle forms between her brows as she eyes me suspiciously.

"It's Sunday," I add. "They close early. And even if you left right now to get there, you'd end up late for work trying to find the right fuse with the kids they got working there. I can get it for you and put it in so you'll be able to have a hot shower when you get home."

Cassidy studies me for a long moment, no doubt doing the driving time math in her head, but I know I'm right, and so does she. "I get out at five today. Do you think you can do it after? I won't be here by the time you get back, and Frankie gets antsy if someone is in the house without me around."

"I can." Popping out the fuses to take with me for reference. "Do you need anything else while I'm there?"

She shifts on her feet, clearly torn between asking me for something else and settling with only accepting my help for the water heater. "Um, my fridge light burnt out. Could you...grab me a new one? They're those funky skinny bulbs."

"Do you have it?"

She nods, sliding past me and down the hall to the kitchen. I follow her lead as she gathers the bulb from beside the sink and hands it to me. "How much do you think the fuses will cost?" she asks, grabbing her purse on the table.

"Don't worry about it," I grumble, flipping the bulb over.

"Butch," she starts. I look at her. "I get you're trying to be nice and everything right now, but...paying for my fuses and light bulbs isn't your responsibility."

"You're right," I grunt. "It's not. And I am trying to be nice right now because I feel like shit about last night. Let me take care of this so I'll be able to sleep tonight."

She sets her purse down. "Fine." Making my way to the door, she follows. "I'm usually back here no later than quarter after."

I open the door to leave. "All right, I'll see you then."

I hop in my truck, placing the fuses and bulb in the cup holder. When I start my truck, I glance up to Cassidy's porch. She's hooking Frankie onto a line outside, watching me with a smile. I freeze, staring at her for a moment too short before she turns away, heading back inside.

Well, damn. That apology just turned into running errands and making repairs for her. It feels...good. It feels *right*. And I don't think I'd have it any other way.

Three hours and three different hardware stores later, I finally got what Cassidy needs. Since when did fuses become a hot commodity? After banging out a few of my own things I needed to get done today, I'm on my way back to Cassidy's before I need to head to my parents' place for Sunday dinner. It's weekly, and generally, mandatory.

I already know I'm going to get shit for being late, but I think I've got a damn good excuse this time.

Pulling in, I catch Cassidy getting out of her car. When she sees me, she smiles. I get out and close the door with her new fuses and fridge bulb in hand.

"Did you find everything okay?" she asks.

"Yeah." *Barely.*

She leads the way up the steps where Frankie sits with a tail that's going crazy. "Hey, chubby baby," she coos, unhooking him from the line and pushing inside.

I follow her in and kick off my boots as she does the same with her sneakers. "Is it okay if I watch how you replace the fuses?" she asks, setting her purse down on the table.

I raise a brow, a little caught off guard. "No problem." Silently surprised, but still not as impressed as her telling me she removed the old water heater and installed this new one all by herself. Seriously, I've been wracking my brain all day on how she did it. They're easily over a hundred pounds and hard as hell to maneuver just right. Especially into this tiny closet.

I walk Cassidy through every step and she looks like she's hanging on my every word, watching my every move. "I'd give it an hour or so and you should be good to take a hot shower."

She closes the closet doors. "Thank you for doing this. I really appreciate it."

I nod, walking back to the kitchen to put the new fridge bulb in. Granted, she could probably do this herself, but I might as well. Opening her fridge, I'm greeted with the sight of it fully stocked with fresh fruit, veggies, and meat.

"You cook a lot?" I ask.

"I do," she says, washing her hands at the sink. "I can cook, but I suck at baking. I always end up burning whatever I try to make, even when I set a timer." She laughs lightly.

Better than me, I think to myself. I always do takeout or drop by my folks' place to steal leftovers or grab a plate to-go.

Frankie waddles over to the open fridge, eagerly sniffing around. Just as he goes to take something out, Cassidy grabs him. "Hey, you little fatty, get out of there."

I chuckle deeply as the light turns on, closing the fridge door. "He's pretty big for a small dog, isn't he?"

Cassidy rolls her eyes with a smile, grabbing some special labeled dog food bag off the counter. "Oh, yeah, he's morbidly obese." She giggles. "Dad used to feed him anything and everything he ate. And even now with being diabetic and on a diet, he's still fat. We try to walk every day when it's not too cold for him the last few years. If you'd believe it, he's lost ten pounds."

My jaw drops. "No way." I point to Frankie. "He was ten pounds bigger than this?"

"Oh, yeah, and he steals food any chance he gets. He's a damn kleptomaniac. It's like his crack. But the biggest mystery has been how he gets on the counter. I still haven't figured it out."

I shake my head with a laugh, crouching down and petting Frankie as he rolls on his back for belly rubs. "How the hell does he get on the counter at this size and with these legs?"

"Your guess is as good as mine." She smiles. "I'll get out of the shower, or come home from work to find him fatter and crying on the counter because he can't get down. That's why when the weather is nice, I leave him out for the day. But it's hard because he doesn't do well with the cold, so he gets to stay in a lot."

"Why don't you get him a crate for when you're gone?"

"Nooo," she coos, kneeling and petting his head. "I couldn't do that to him. He's always been so good, never makes a mess or chews anything. He'd end up crying his little heart out if I did that to him."

Cassidy stands, gesturing to the stove. "I was going to make chicken alfredo tonight. You're welcome to stay if you want. Since you won't let me pay you for the fuses."

Dammit. I stand. "I'd love to, but I can't." I hate the words even leaving my mouth. "My folks do a mandatory Sunday dinner every week."

She smiles kindly. "That's nice."

"It can be." I scratch my bearded chin. "I should probably get going actually."

"Okay." She follows me to the door and out onto the porch. "Thanks again for helping me today."

I nod, going down the steps before I turn back to her. "If you don't mind me asking, does your brother ever help you out around here? I know you said you installed that hot water tank yourself, but didn't he help ya out with it?"

She sighs. "No. I do everything around here. Garrett's more of a...come and go guest. I can't even get him to take the trash out or mow the grass when I ask. So, yeah, I do it all."

I can't help but scowl at that. I take out my wallet and remove one of my business cards with my cell phone number on it, handing it to her. "If you ever need anything or have any trouble, you can call me."

She takes the card, looks it over and back up to me with a small smile. "Thank you."

Heading for my truck, Cassidy stands on the porch watching me as I leave. And I can't help but grin like a maniac when I drive out of sight.

Did I just make right on the cup, fight, *and* get in to be her go-to when she needs help?

Because I sure as hell hope so.

Nine.

Cassidy

"HE CHANGED YOUR FUSES," Alison repeats, helping me stock the display. "Is that some kind of euphemism for something sexual I haven't heard about?"

I can't help but laugh at that. "No, Alison, it means he helped me change my *fuses* for the hot water tank when they blew. He also gave me his card and told me if I needed anything, to call him."

"Oh, now *that* is hot," Janice chimes in, leaning over the counter with a dreamy sigh. "There's nothing sexier than a man who can fix things. And Butch can build *and* fix." She fans herself at the thought.

And she's not wrong.

"I mean, *sure*, it's kind of hot, but that doesn't make up for Saturday night," Alison deadpans, a heated scowl on her face. "He went after your brother rather than checking on you. And being your voice of reason here, need I remind you how upset you were about that very fact."

I sigh. "First of all, I don't remember crying about that to you. Second, why would I be upset he didn't check on me? We're hardly even friends."

Except...are we? The more I think about him and the time we've spent together over the last few weeks, how easy it's been to be around him. And how, dare I say, *good* I feel when I am with him, I suppose we are. Friends.

"Y'all are sounding pretty *friendly* to me if he's changing your, quote: *fuses*," Alison says, exaggerating air quotes with her fingers.

"I'd be upset if he didn't check on me either," Janice reasons. "You spent the entire night laughing, drinking, and having a great time. You said it was going great until Garrett ruined everything."

I sigh. "Yeah, it was."

"And," Alison starts, "he came to apologize after, which is proof alone it was screwed up that he went after Garrett and not straight to you. Cass, when I pulled up, you were shaking. That's how upset you were."

"Well, I think he likes you," Peggy finally speaks up, sealing her statement with a sip of her morning coffee.

I snort. "How did you get to that conclusion?"

Peggy smiles brightly, setting down her coffee with a look of triumph. "I'm glad you asked, my dear Cassidy."

"Oh, boy, this is going to be good." Alison laughs.

"I ran into Butch's mother, Julie Montgomery, yesterday evening at the Quick-Mart. And I must say, she knows about you," Peggy announces. My eyes widen. "My point exactly. Apparently, Butch was not only *late* to Sunday dinner, but he had quite a few words to say to his family about you installing a water heater by yourself."

"Wha—What did he say?" I ask in shock.

Peggy hums. "She didn't say, she was making a quick run for milk for Lily's boy. But she wanted me to tell you she says, hello."

"Ooo, hello, huh?" Janice snickers. "She already knows."

"Knows what?" Alison demands, practically on the edge of her seat.

Peggy muses, "That her son has a crush."

I scoff loudly. "Butch does *not* have a crush on me. We're not in high school. He's thirty-four years old."

"Hey, you said that wasn't too old for you," Alison exclaims.

Janice adds, "It's not. Billy and I are thirteen years apart, and it's perfect."

I roll my eyes so hard my head begins to pound. "Janice, don't even go there. You complain about Billy like he's the hardest stain to get out of your carpet."

"I do, don't I." She laughs. "But that doesn't mean I don't love him to bits."

Peggy holds me with a stern gaze. "I think you should give him a chance. The poor boy is clearly hurting for someone in his life. He's been single ever since Mary was unfaithful to him. I heard he even had a ring for her—threw it in the woodchipper at work. Joe told me all about it years ago from Stanley Hall. That was *not* a good day on the mountain."

"Wait," I say, pausing. "Mary Thompson? When were they together?"

"Oh, you were away at college," Janice tells me. "They were together for two years before someone caught her cheating with a younger fella in Billings. That was five years ago. No one's seen Butch with a woman since. Apart from at the bar."

"Maybe that's why he asked you to go there." Alison attempts miserably to put the pieces together. "He wanted a quicky in the back alley."

I sigh. "No, Alison, he didn't want a *quicky*. I was sitting right there when Lauren Bishop tried to take him out back. She flat out offered him a blow job in front of everyone."

Janice scoffs, shaking her head. "Unbelievable. You know, she had chlamydia last year. Gave it to Anthony Smith who ended up giving it to his pregnant wife."

I cringe. "Jesus."

"Butch didn't do it, did he?" Alison asks, disgusted.

"No. He told her to get lost. I guess it was the second time that night by the time I got there."

"Because he likes *you*," Peggy says as a matter of fact. "You know, I wonder if he's even been with anyone recently. What do you think, Janice? Think we should call up Roger and see if he knows?"

Janice starts to take out her phone, but I stop her immediately. "No one is calling anyone," I snap. "Butch will be here any minute, and I don't need you all staring and making him uncomfortable."

Alison snickers, Janice smiles, and Peggy wiggles her eyebrows at me. "Since when do you mind if Butch Montgomery is uncomfortable?"

"Peggy," I scold, eyeing Butch's truck pull in.

"He's here," Wade announces from his spot by the window. "You hens back off. Cassidy deserves a good man who can change her fuses properly."

"Oh, *god*," I groan, covering my face in complete embarrassment as they start to laugh and move about casually. They all fail miserably attempting to appear busy, but still close enough to eavesdrop.

Kill me now.

I get his extra-large coffee and take a deep breath as the bell chimes. I turn back to the counter to a towering, scowling mountain of a man. "Good morning," I say, placing his coffee down in front of him.

"Morning," he grunts, tossing cash down on the counter. "I'll try one of those sugar cookies today."

I nod, gathering his two breakfast sandwiches and cookie.

While I'm packing them up, he asks, "How'd you make out with the water heater?"

Alison starts to snicker and I shoot her a glaring side-eye before responding, "Good." I set the bag down. "Water was hotter than

I've ever gotten it. Made me wonder if they were slowly dying out beforehand."

"It's possible. You should probably check your entire circuit. Make sure you don't have a short somewhere."

I exhale, cashing him out. "I'll add it to the list."

His brow furrows. "You've got a list?"

"Yeah, the Get-To-It-When-I-Can list." And if it's even possible, Butch scowls harder. "Doesn't...everyone have a list?" I ask slowly, handing him his change.

He huffs, tossing the change in the tip jar. "What's at the top of your list?"

I shrug. "There's a roof leak over Garrett's room, but Mr. Finley helped me patch it temporarily a few weeks ago."

"Patch it with what?" he presses further.

"Plywood."

Butch scoffs loud enough that he doesn't need to use words to tell me what he thinks of that idea. "I'll take a look at it for you," he tells me like it's *not* up for discussion. He snatches his coffee and to-go bag from the counter rather aggressively and stalks off without saying another word.

The whole coffee shop is dead silent as I watch him get into his truck and pull off toward the mountain. That was...odd.

"Sooo, you still going to say he doesn't have a thing for you?" Alison asks with a beaming smile.

"Plywood," Wade mutters with a shake of his head. "I tell you what, Bob Finley is a damn dumbass."

Well, shoot. I didn't think plywood was a bad idea. And considering I hate heights; it was more or less whatever Bob was willing to do for me at the time.

"He's just being nice," I say, internally questioning everything I've ever known or heard about Butch Montgomery on top of everything he's ever said to me.

"Nice enough to change your *fuses* and patch up your *leak*." Alison laughs.

"What'd you write on his cup today?" Peggy asks curiously.

"*Expect nothing, appreciate everything.*"

"Oh, that's fitting." She smiles knowingly.

Janice hums. "You know, I bet my wedding dress would fit you, if you'd like to take a look at it."

I exaggerate a groan, and they all laugh. But for some reason, I can't seem to wipe this smile off my face. Because as big of a dick as Butch has been in the past, he's already done more for me than anyone has in a very, very long time.

Ten.

Cassidy

I GLIDE THE DIGITAL pen over my tablet, aiming to create a more wistful look to the 'Y' in *you* for the *Thank You* card I'm working on—until Frankie nudges my hand and forces the pen off the screen.

I sigh as he stares at me with those big puppy dog eyes. "Frankie..."

He nudges my hand again.

"Fine." I give in, setting my tablet to the side and giving him long body pets. He stretches and flops on his back beside me for his desired belly rubs. I continue petting him, leaning my head back against the cushioned patio loveseat I splurged on last spring. It's my favorite spot to brainstorm and work on my cards when the weather is nice.

I yawn, checking the time on my phone and wondering what I should do for dinner tonight. Part of me doesn't want to bother making anything for just me—a package of Pop-Tarts will serve the same purpose. It's not like I have anyone to cook for or enjoy it with.

Not since Dad passed and Garrett left me here all alone.

I take a deep breath, my eyes burning as I fight the emotion welling to the surface. Frankie flips over, his ears perking as he sits up beside me. Reaching for my tablet to clear my head with some art therapy, I sniffle. "What is it, Frankster, you hear the chipmunk under the porch again?"

The distinct rumble of a truck pulling in has my head lifting and my gaze locking with the last person I expected to see.

Frankie yips and hops down, his whole body wiggles with excitement as Butch gets out and slams his truck door behind him. He grabs something from the back before making his way toward me.

He sets a bag on the bottom step. "How's it goin'?"

"Good." I set my tablet off to the side and unfold my legs from under me. The oversized, baggie T-shirt and athletic shorts I'm wearing shows I've been home for hours being lazy, meanwhile Butch is dressed exactly how I saw him this morning. Except now he's covered in sweat and sawdust with a hefty amount of dirt sticking to his brow.

He looks like he just got done with a hard day's work, and...he chose to come here?

"Did we—"

"Ready to tackle that list of yours?" he asks.

I pause on the top step, gazing at him with a mixture of confusion and uncertainty. Is he serious? We only just spoke—barely—about my list of things I need to do around here *this* morning. And now he's here? For me?

Butterflies flutter low in my belly and I can't help the smile stretching my face. "Really?"

He opens his arms wide. "I'm all yours."

I fight the urge to launch myself into those very arms and settle for a giddy bounce that brings a wide, devastatingly handsome smile to his face. If there's one thing I've learned about Butch in the last few weeks; when he says something, he means it.

Hands on my hips, I squint up into the sun, trying to make out the broad form standing on the roof of my trailer.

"Heads up," he hollers, tossing the flimsy plywood piece into the yard beside me. Frankie immediately hobbles down the steps to investigate, sniffing around. He's been just as enamored with the process as I have.

Butch starts to make his way back down the ladder. "All set up here," he tells me, tossing an empty can of roof sealant into the garbage bin.

I gnaw on my bottom lip as I watch the shirtless, tatted mountain man break down the ladder he brought and toss it back into the bed of his truck. The sun is out and it's warm—likely hot up there on the roof. Hot enough for the delicious tan of Butch's skin to be rippled with sweat in every thick carve of muscle he has. He's practically shimmering like a mountain god in the setting sun.

I shift on my bare feet in the grass, ogling his tight ass in those Carhartts as he throws his shirt back on and bends down to pick up the tool bag he dropped by the porch. He turns to look at me and my stomach flops. He runs one of those big hands over his sweaty forehead and into his hair, slicking it back and making it look even darker.

"Let's have a look at that ceiling," he says.

All I do is stare. He's so...sexy.

He's a mountain of sex appeal and I want nothing more than to climb him in this moment.

He raises a brow at me, the very corner of his lip lifting at my obvious objectifying of him. My cheeks heat and I shake off whatever mountain trance he just put me in and hop up the steps. "What, um—oh, are you thirsty?" I ramble as I open the door.

"A drink would be nice," he grunts, kicking off his boots at the door.

Frankie waddles into the cool living room, heading straight for his spot on the couch.

I grab two bottles of water from the fridge, handing one to Butch. "Sorry, no beer. I try not to keep it in the house."

"It's all good," he mumbles and breaks the seal, tipping his head back and chugging half straight away. I watch his strong neck work, the way his throat moves as he swallows, the heavy bob of his Adam's apple. I absently wonder what it would be like to—

"This your brother's room?" he asks, making his way toward Garrett's door at the front of the trailer.

I set my water on the table, hurrying after him. "Yes, but—" He pushes open the door without a second thought. "—I don't think he'll be happy we're in here," I finish with a sigh.

Butch scoffs. "He should be thankful I'm even checking for mold."

My eyes widen. "Mold?"

He merely grunts in response, moving further into the tight space.

I stand off to the side, watching Butch inspect the tear in the popcorn ceiling surrounded by brown water stains. It looks awful, and I can't help the wave of embarrassment that washes over me.

Life in a trailer park isn't luxurious, it's simple living. You make it what you can. I've always tried to create a comfortable space for my brother and me, especially after Mom left and Dad passed. Garrett hasn't always been the tidiest and he doesn't have much in here aside from a dresser, an old-school TV that should be trashed, and a twin bed that's far too small for a grown man.

I spare a glance at my brother's only beloved possession. His guitar is propped in the corner of the room. Cleaned, tuned, and dusted even though it hasn't been touched in two years. My chest tightens at the memory of how far gone my brother has fallen, and how badly I wish I could bring him back to me.

Hopefully, this little repair to his room will—I don't know, convince him to come home more often and...

Stay away from the bottle, I think to myself.

I sigh, staring up at the ceiling as Butch shoves Garrett's bed further toward the far wall. "It's dry," he says, grabbing his tool bag and setting it on the bed. "I can patch it with some spackle now, or I can get a piece of drywall to cut this damaged area out and replace it another day."

I shrug. "Whatever you think is best."

He takes out a brand-new container of spackle and a putty knife, eyeing the spot up for repair. "I think I can get it lookin' right with the texture up here," he says, flipping the tool in his hand. He peers over at me. "If it looks like hell after, we can try option two."

I give him a small smile. "Sounds good."

Butch gets to work on the repair, reaching up and slapping a wad of white paste and spreading it gently.

"Thank you again for doing this," I start, crossing my arms and leaning against the open door frame. "I know I've already said it, but I really appreciate it."

"Don't mention it," he huffs, focused on the task at hand.

"If you ever need help on the mountain, let me know."

"Oh, yeah?" Butch chuckles, glancing over at me. "You know how to work a yarder by chance?"

I exaggerate a scoff. "Oh, for sure."

"Do you know what a yarder *does*?"

"Yeah…it's, uh, one of those log pulley things, right?"

His eyes sparkle with mirth as his smile grows. "It's a system of cables that pull the logs up the mountain to the collection site. So, yeah, a log pulley thing." Butch's laugh is so deep and contagious, I can't help but join him.

He finishes up quicker than I expected. Taking a step back, he ushers me further into the room. "How's that look?"

I inspect the freshly spackled area that looked hideous a moment ago. The white is brighter than the rest of the ceiling, but unless you're looking closely, you wouldn't know it was patched at a passing glance. "It's perfect," I admit. "Five stars."

He chuckles, scraping the putty knife on the side of the container before closing it up. "I'll have to let Rhett and Levi know I'm encroaching on their construction business."

When my eyes meet his, I smile. "Thank you."

Hefting his tool bag off the bed he takes a step closer to me until we're a breath from touching. I breathe in deep, inhaling his leftover cologne mixed with his natural musk and sweat. If the heat from his body wasn't already drawing me in, that deep yearning in his dark eyes right now would do the trick.

"Are you hungry?" I ask.

Please say yes. Please say yes.

"Starving."

I beam. "Did you want to stay for dinner? I've got everything to make my grandma's famous homemade meatball subs." I don't even give him a chance to respond before I'm spinning on my heels for the kitchen. I originally bought it all hoping Garrett would be home a few days this week. His birthday is Thursday and we always do something together—Granny's meatballs have been his favorite since he could chew.

But Butch is here *now*. And I can always go back to the store.

I flick on the oven and dive into the fridge, gathering everything I need. The scraping of the dining chair on the cheap linoleum flooring has me peeking over my shoulder as Butch takes a seat at the small breakfast nook table. "Anything homemade sounds good to me."

"Well, you'll love these," I say. "I try to make them at least once a month. They're Garrett's favorite."

He nods, leaning back in the chair with a creak as he folds his thick forearms over his chest. He watches me as I cook, prepping the hamburger meat with a slew of spices and mixing them in by hand.

"Why no beer?"

"Hm?"

"You said you didn't have beer because you don't like it in the house," he adds. "Why's that?"

"Garrett will just drink it all anyway." I shrug. "Besides, on the off chance he is here, I prefer my brother sober. He's more..." I trail off, trying to find the right words to explain the complexity that is *Garrett Clark*.

"Tolerable?"

I shake my head with a laugh. "He's more himself, if that makes sense."

Glancing back over my shoulder, he asks, "Has he always been a heavy drinker?"

"No, not always," I say, rolling a hefty wad of seasoned meat between my hands into a fat meatball. "He picked it up a bit when we found out Dad was sick. Everything went to hell after that. Mom ran off with some guy she barely knew, days before Dad started treatment. I finished college and came home to help where I could—cooking, cleaning, paying the bills, taking care of Dad."

"Your brother didn't help?"

"He did." I set the half a dozen meatballs in the cast-iron skillet and pop them in the oven to bake for a bit. "In the beginning, Garrett was right there with me. Running Dad to appointments, taking odd jobs around town to help pay off the piling medical bills, tag teaming who stayed up with him throughout the night just so he wasn't alone and in pain—he was there for all of it. Until it got close to the end." I wash my hands and turn to face Butch watching me as I dry them with the dish towel. "He started to...disassociate, is what they call it. He distanced himself little by little, helped less and less. He didn't want to be a part of Dad's end. He still can't accept the fact he's gone."

"And that's when he picked up drinking?"

I nod, tossing the towel on the counter behind me. "They were close. Really close. My dad said he understood and to let it be, but...it just didn't seem fair. Our father was dying and he couldn't handle it. So I was stuck with everything—the medical bills, the trailer, the grief. I still am."

Butch shakes his head lightly. "Why'd you stay? I mean, after everything was said and done, why stay?"

I take a deep breath. That is the burning question, isn't it? Alison asks me all the time, and I get it, it doesn't make sense to a lot of people. Not after everything Garrett's put me through. "He's my brother, Butch, he's all I have left." A faint smile ghosts over my lips. "It might sound stupid, but I still have faith he'll come around. He just needs time. We all do, sometimes."

Butch is silent as I finish the meatballs on the stovetop and warm up the sauce, which is fine by me. It's just nice knowing he's here with me. It feels...good having him here. And as I plate up a small salad beside the ten-inch toasted meatball sub slathered in red sauce and topped with several slices of melted mozzarella, I'm suddenly nervous about what he'll think of it.

And what he thinks of me...

I set his plate down in front of him and smile with a gracious wave over the plate. "*Voila!* Granny's famous meatball sub."

Butch rubs his hands together with a grin and dives right in. "Mmm," he moans over a mouthful. "This is—" he pauses, dramatically closing his eyes and chewing before looking up at me. "You're amazing."

I practically preen at his praise. Quickly taking the chair beside him with my plate, we eat and chat about everything and nothing at all. He tells me about his family and how close he is with his brother, Duke. The conversation flows so effortlessly that I lose track of time before I finally notice it's quarter after nine.

"I've got it," I say, taking the dirty plates from Butch as he stands. "It's getting late, you've probably got an early morning." I know I do.

He grunts, ignoring the out I just gave him and helping clean up anyway. I bite my lip to keep from laughing. I would've never thought I'd enjoy having him here this much—and how bad I don't want him to go. Not yet.

We're quiet as I wash the dishes and hand them to him to dry and place on the rack beside me. *Do I say something? Is it weird if I do or is it weirder if I don't? Is this a date? No, it almost feels more intimate than a date. It's more than that. It's—*

"What you got for me tomorrow?"

Confused, I look up at him towering beside me, his stern gaze focused in front of him. "What do you mean?"

"Your list," he grumbles, setting the pan he was drying aside and finally meeting my gaze. "I told you I'd help you out with whatever you needed. I meant it. You've got enough going on and I've got the time."

"You work hard all day, Butch," I reason.

"So do you."

I give him an exasperated look. He won't win this argument with me. "You're a blue-collar man. I know what it takes to do the work you do day in and day out. It's not fair of me to ask you to come here and do mundane chores after a long day on the mountain."

He tosses the dish towel on the counter and turns to fully face me, his body briefly brushing against mine as he takes a deep breath. "I wish you would."

Stunned, I gape at him for a moment as my heart swoons its own race.

He does?

"You—" I'm cut short by the blaring ring of my phone. I spare a glimpse at it sitting beside the sink. It's Alison.

"I should get going," Butch tells me, moving toward the door to put his boots back on.

"I'll walk you out," I start to say when my phone stops ringing only to immediately start up again. She's going to blow me up with back-to-back calls until I answer, isn't she? I snatch my phone and swipe to answer. "Can I call you back—"

She squeals, "Tanner asked me out!"

"Tanner Wright asked you out?"

Butch looks up at me as he laces his boots up. "Asked who out?"

I hold the phone away from my ear. "Alison."

"Yeah?" she asks through the phone, still giddy on cloud nine.

"No, no. I wasn't talking to you. I was—"

"Then who are you talking to? Is Garrett home?" she questions.

I sigh. "Can you hold on a second?" I say, muting the phone as Butch grabs his tool bag from the floor. I don't want him to leave like this. He's giving me the same look Frankie gives me when I deny him a treat after powering through one of our walks.

"The faucet in the bathroom drips and the showerhead is loose," I start, and I swear his eyes sparkle as I list off several more chores. "I'm sure you noticed the gutters need to be cleaned and the siding in the back needs to be power washed badly. And I'd love to clean out the shed. There's so much junk in there that hasn't been touched in forever. I couldn't even tell you what kind of random tools and things my dad hoarded over the years."

"All right," he says, looking practically thrilled. "Is it the showerhead itself or where it's attached to the wall that's loose?"

"All of the above," I say. "I wouldn't mind looking at new ones. Maybe we can go together later this week and you can help me pick one out?"

Alison's voice drifts from the phone in my hand, asking what the hell I'm doing and that she needs to speak to me *now*.

"Do you still have the card I gave you?" he asks, and I nod. "Text me and we'll figure out a time. I'll see you tomorrow?"

The way he says it comes out like a question. And I love that he sounds unsure, even after everything I just said. I smile, moving toward him. "I'll see you tomorrow, Butch. Goodnight." I lift on the tips of my toes, my lips brushing against his scruffy cheek in a soft peck. "Drive safe." My lips tingle as I drop back down to my feet.

"Text me," he repeats, clearing his throat as he turns quickly. He hesitates before he finally opens the door. "Night, Cassidy."

I watch him from the door as he gets in his truck and drives away. He didn't want to leave just as much as I didn't want him to leave.

But he did. Why? Is this how he is when he picks women up from the bar? There's no way. So why now? *This is different*, I think to myself. I can feel it. Garrett always says I have a shitty sixth sense when it comes to men—is that what's happening now?

Am I wrong about Butch?

The questions rattle in my head as I close the door and Alison's piercing squeal that *Tanner is texting her* reminds me she's still on the phone. Before I take her off mute, I make sure to text Butch to let me know when he gets home. And it feels so right when I do.

Eleven.

Butch

"Remind me again what you need all this for?" Rhett asks for the third time since I showed up at the lumber yard where he and Levi run their construction company.

He's either playing dumb or he still doesn't believe me.

"I already told you," I grunt, lifting the commercial-grade power washer onto the tailgate and pushing it into the bed of my truck. "You got an extra hose I can borrow with this?"

Rhett crosses his arms over his chest, eyeing me suspiciously. "If the Clarks needed roof repairs—why didn't they just call and book a consult? Might've been a few weeks, but Levi or I could've squeezed them in."

I huff and stomp over to the garden hose attached to the side of the outbuilding. I don't get why he's so butt-hurt over this. "She didn't ask, I offered," I say, unscrewing the hose and tossing it in the back. I didn't see one at Cassidy's, and we didn't find one when we cleaned out her father's junk-filled shed yesterday.

Monday night after I left, we texted for a while, making plans for the week. I'd never stayed up later on a Monday than I did that night. On Tuesday, I picked her up after work and we went to Andy's Hardware to get her a new showerhead and seals for the bathroom sink. We ended up grabbing takeout and went back to her place. I installed the new showerhead and had her sink fixed in record time just so I could spend my time focused on her—I couldn't even tell you when I ended up leaving. Wednesday, we cleaned the shed out, and she cooked another amazing meal. And today, we're supposed to do the gutters and siding.

It's been nearly a full day since I've seen her, and I'm itching like a madman to get over there. She took the day off today for her brother's birthday. Which means I didn't get to see her at the coffee shop this morning, souring my mood for the rest of the day.

She was hesitant the last time we spoke about doing anything tonight, worried her brother might be home, but she hasn't heard from him. And I haven't heard from her since late last night.

All the more reason why I need to get my ass over there and be with her.

"Ahh, I get it now." My brother grins. "Duke mentioned something about you and Cassidy starting a thing."

I huff, annoyed that my damn brother couldn't keep his mouth shut. "We're not..." I trail off. Are we starting something? It sure feels like it. I haven't stopped thinking about her for a second all day—all week, if I'm being honest here. I even ditched work early today to catch Rhett and pick up this thing.

"Sure you're not," Rhett muses. "Just didn't think you'd be here on a Thursday after five borrowing a power washer is all."

I ignore him, getting in my truck. "Thanks."

"If you need help, holler," he calls, laughter in his voice as I slam the door shut.

I head straight for Cassidy's. My mind racing. Mostly over how we'll be ending the night tonight. Not that I'm expecting anything from her, but…I won't be leaving unless she outright tells me to.

The idea of spending the night with her has my cock stirring. I shift in my seat, wondering if she'll let me take her out to dinner tonight.

And have *her* for dessert.

By the time I pull into the park, it's a quarter to six. I've got maybe two hours of daylight left—if I'm lucky—to get this done. And as confident as I've been all day with my plan for the rest of the night, doubt creeps in as I approach her short drive.

My brow furrows. Her Jeep is parked in her usual spot, but there are four other vehicles in her yard blocking her in that I don't recognize.

As I park off to the side, I kill the engine and wait. Her brother has to be home. It's his birthday…but she didn't text me not to come? She hasn't said anything since last night. Should I go in or text her I'm here? Should we reschedule?

Fuck. This sucks.

I tap my thumb on the steering wheel, trying to figure out what the hell I want to do here when I hear yelling. I look around, unsure of where it came from. The trailers in here are so damn close together it could've been from any one of them. Loud, blaring music starts up, muffling the shouting.

It's then, I realize, it *is* coming from her place.

I get out a split second later, taking long strides up to the porch. The blasting rock music does nothing to cover Frankie's high-pitched barking and a man shouting. When I hear Cassidy yelling in return, I slam a fist on the door. More like a pounding demand than a welcoming knock as my blood starts to boil.

If this asshole upset her again, I swear I'll—

The door swings open and my chest cinches painfully. She looks...exhausted. Her eyes are puffy and bloodshot as fresh tears stream down her cheeks with Frankie trembling in her arms. He yips in my direction, trying to reach out and greet me.

Cassidy's lower lip wobbles as she peers up at me. "Butch..."

The way she says my name is like a meat cleaver to the heart. This is the second time I've seen her cry now, but this feels different. I can't handle seeing her this heartbroken and not do something about it.

She's mine to protect. And I'm not leaving here without her.

Cassidy must sense what I'm thinking as I glare over her head and into the trailer at her back. At least seven people are lingering between the kitchen and living room watching me. And I can tell from here—the place is trashed. How long have they been partying for? All night and all day? My jaw ticks as I lock eyes with Garrett and the nearly empty beer bottle in his hand.

He looks like shit, and I'd love nothing more than to give him a black eye to match the rest of him.

"I'm sorry," she whispers, bringing my attention back to the angel of a woman in front of me. "I forgot to text you, um…now's not a good time."

I take a step closer, crowding her with my body. I reach out, wiping away a stray tear before it falls. She leans into me as Frankie rubs against me, shaking like a leaf. The poor little guy. "You've got two choices here," I growl, my anger rising. "I stay and beat your brother's fucking ass, or you come with me right now. Either way, I'm not leaving you here alone."

A brief war wages behind those deep ocean eyes before she nods faintly. *Good.*

I nod sternly in return, my hand going to her arm to steer her inside. "Let's get your stuff."

Garrett barges forward as someone finally turns the music down. "What the hell do you think you're doing here, Montgomery?"

Cassidy stops, now pinned between us with Garrett at her front and me at her back. I wait to see if she has anything to say, but she doesn't. I don't want to get in the middle of whatever family shit they've got going on, but when she leans away from her brother and back into me, I know she needs me right now.

"Back off, Clark," I say, attempting to keep my voice level to show I'm not here for a fight.

"You weren't invited, *prick*. Get out of my house," he shouts, slurring his words.

I grit my teeth, trying to keep it cool for Cassidy's sake no matter how bad I want to shove my fist down his throat. I take a deep breath and guide her in my arms through the kitchen to head down the hall when I'm roughly grabbed from behind. I quickly release my hold on Cassidy so I don't bring her back with me as I spin around and knock a pair of hands from me.

Garrett's in my face a second later, pushing his chest into mine. I don't budge. "You got something else you need to get off your chest there, Clark? Because if you're lookin' for another fight, you're not gonna get one from me."

He studies me with dark, glossy eyes. There's no telling how many he's had, and I'm not sure how this is about to play out. "Leave," he grinds out, his breath reeking of booze.

I press back against him. "I'm not going anywhere."

A few idiots sitting on the couch start to stand. And just when I think we're about to have a real problem here, Cassidy takes my hand and places a strap of some kind in it. I turn, looking down at her and the light duffle bag she's handed me. I didn't even notice her walk away. Too distracted by her brother and whatever the hell he has going on in his head right now.

"I need a few more things," she whispers. "And stuff for Frankie."

I tighten my grip on the bag as she slips between her brother and me. Still clutching Frankie to her chest—which can't be easy considering his size—she hands me his dog food off the counter and reaches into the fridge for a compact medical cooler.

Garrett's eyes track her every move. He must have had a good bit to drink because it's clear he's trying to figure out what's going on. Unfortunately, he catches on. "That's right, Cass. Following in her footsteps now, huh?"

What is he even talking about?

His sister ignores him, hooking the leash to Frankie and handing him to me. "Can you take him to my car? I've got a few more things I want to grab."

"You're blocked in," I say, snarling at the sea of drunks watching us. Not a single one of them is in any shape to be picking up a set of keys let alone moving their car. "We'll figure something out tomorrow."

She sighs. "Okay..."

"I'll be right back." I wait for a beat, glaring at Garrett to do something as she goes back down the hall. He does nothing, just stands there with his brows cast down and sways. I quickly head out to my truck and put Frankie in the front seat, tossing everything else in the backseat before going back inside.

As I walk in, Cassidy comes into view at the end of the hallway carrying a shotgun and a small fire safe you'd use to put important documents in. I keep a stern expression, not wanting to show my surprise at how little trust she truly has in her brother.

He notices, too. "Where the hell you goin' with that?" he barks, taking a step forward and accidentally tripping on the leg of one of the wooden chairs at the table beside him. He kicks the chair and stumbles. I reach out and grip his upper arm, holding him upright.

A moment later he gains his footing, yanking his arm away. But his focus isn't on me, it's on Cassidy as she speaks. "You want the trailer, Garrett? Fine. You can have it," she snaps, fresh tears streaming down her face. "But you are *not* taking everything Dad left us and selling it. I won't let you."

"Why not?" he demands. "Isn't that what you're doing? Cleaning up the place to sell it right out from under me. What? You didn't think I wouldn't notice all the shit you got rid of in Dad's shed?"

Cassidy shakes her head and goes to the front door. "I'm done arguing with you, Garrett." She pauses in the doorway, glancing back at him. "I'm *done.*"

Rage flashes in her brother's eyes and I hold out an arm to block him from taking another step in her direction. "You think I give a shit?" he shouts, waving his hands wildly as she steps outside. "That's right—pack up and leave just like she did when the goin' gets rough," he spits, forcing a laugh. "Mom would be so fucking proud."

"Enough," I grind, pushing him rougher than I should, to the point his back slams against the fridge with a shake.

What can I say, he brings out the worst in me.

I shake my head to myself and step toward the door. I need to stop wasting energy on this prick and focus on what matters—Cassidy. But he's her brother, and what matters to her, matters to me.

I hesitate at the door, the knob tight in my hand and ready to slam shut behind me. My eyes find Garrett's, and for once I'd venture to say there's genuine regret in them. "I'm not one for motivational speeches, but I'll tell you this—get your shit together, Clark," I seethe, wanting my words to sting. "Your sister needs you around more than you need to finish off that bottle of liquor, you hear me?"

He stiffens then, slamming a hand on the counter to keep himself upright. I've never seen someone this far gone before. "You don't know what you're talkin' 'bout," he mutters.

I gesture around the room at the half-dozen pairs of eyes watching us. "You think a single one of these fuckers gives a shit if you drink yourself into a hole in the ground? They don't. The sooner you realize Cassidy is all you've got left, the better off you'll be." I pause, waiting to see if he has anything to come back at me with, and when he doesn't, I add, "When you get your head out of your ass—call me. There's a treatment facility in Billings I've heard good things about."

His eyes glaze over and I can tell he's on the verge of tears—it's the same look Cassidy gets when she's upset. *Good. He needs to feel at his lowest before he can commit to making a change*, I think to myself as I close the door behind me and make my way down the porch steps.

I look up to Frankie watching me from the passenger side window, but not Cassidy. Her head is in her hands and I can tell I'm in for it tonight.

Whatever she wants, she'll have it. However she wants it, she'll get it. Anything she needs, I'll make sure she doesn't even need to think twice.

I'm here now.

And I'm not going anywhere.

Twelve.

Cassidy

I DON'T STOP CRYING fat, ugly tears until we've left the trailer park and fully passed the coffee shop. I sniffle and stare out the window, unsure where we're going. Well...I have an idea, I'm just having a hard time grasping it.

Butch hasn't said much since he got in and started driving—nothing, in fact. I drag my gaze over to him with Frankie sitting in his lap and his nose pressed to the driver's side window leaving wet nose smears all over it. I smile faintly at the sight—a big, growly mountain man with a fat sausage between his legs.

A giggle escapes me at the double meaning.

Butch's head snaps in my direction. His brows furrowed deep into the scowl that drove me crazy weeks ago. Now, it just makes me feel...cared for. Funny how perspectives can change like that.

He turns back to the road. "I'd rather hear you laughing at me than listen to you cry any longer," he grunts.

I lean my head against the seat. "Sorry."

"Don't be," he says. "When did he get home?"

"Late last night," I say. "After midnight they all started trickling in."

"Why didn't you call me?"

I shrug a shoulder and roll my head to stare out the window as the tears threaten yet again.

"I don't want you thinking you can't call me—*ever*," he says sternly.

"It's not that," I whisper, roughly wiping away the useless tears. "I...didn't think it was going to end like it did, I guess. I just wanted... I don't know." I sigh. What *was* I hoping for? That all my brother's stupid friends would leave and we'd spend Garrett's birthday just the two of us watching movies and hanging out like old times?

I start to cry again.

Butch lets out a deep, frustrated growl, his grip on the steering wheel so tight his knuckles begin to turn white. "I'll fuckin' kill him."

I shake my head, sniffling as I dig through my bag for my phone. "No, it's fine. I-I'm fine. I just—"

"Stop defending him, Cass," he bellows and I freeze, glancing over at him. He spares me a brief side-eye before focusing on the road. "I get it, I really do. If it was any one of my siblings, I'd feel the same. But at some point, you have to separate yourself from his bullshit. It's not doing you any good."

I take a wobbly breath. He's not wrong, but he's not entirely right either. "I can't just abandon him."

"You're not," he says, his tone steady and reasoning. "Think of it this way—be his backup."

"His backup?"

He nods. "He'll call on you when he's ready—when he needs your support. Be there for him but at a distance. Like my father always says, *you have to learn to wipe your own ass some time*."

A burst of laughter explodes from my chest. "What does that even mean?"

Butch chuckles. "It *means*, he's a big boy and he can handle himself. And when he's ready, you'll be there waiting without the added hurt between the two of ya."

My laughter turns to smiling tears as I reach over and touch his arm. He pulls his arm back to take my hand instead. I give it a little squeeze. "Thank you," I whisper. "For showing up and, well, just being you."

A wide grin spreads across his face. "Think that's the first time anyone's ever thanked me for being myself. You'd be surprised to know, it's usually the opposite."

That's the least bit surprising. I smile while still holding his hand over the center console when my phone pings a few times with new text messages. Reluctantly, I let go of his steady, comforting hold to check who it is.

Alison: *OMG! Yes, of course, you can stay here tonight.*

Alison: *Oh, wait... Frankie, too? I'm sorry, Cass. My apartment is no dogs allowed.*

Alison: *We can try to sneak him in?*

Crap. I forgot I texted her when I got out to Butch's truck, asking if Frankie and I could come crash with her for the weekend. Or at least until things blow over with Garrett. *He just needs space*, I reinforce to myself, *like Butch said.*

Suddenly, I start to worry about what I *am* going to do. Butch never said Frankie could come with us, or stay at his house—if he was even offering we go *to* his house. I assumed. And now...could I even go back home with Garrett and all those people watching us interact like some sort of live reality TV show? No. Absolutely not.

"Who is it?"

"I asked Alison if I could stay with her, but, um, I guess I can't."

Butch tenses with a heavy hold on the steering wheel. "I told you; you can stay with me."

"You never actually said—"

"Then I'm saying it now," he deadpans. "You're staying with me until your brother can get his head on straight. I'm not letting you go back there. And besides, the place was fucking trashed."

I blow out a calming breath, not wanting to cry again since it seems to bother him so much. Last night was like a frat party in the living room, and what Butch caught a glimpse of, was the place *after* I attempted to clean up and kick people out. Which is about when the fighting began and Butch showed up. "And Frankie?"

"What about him?"

"Is it okay if he comes, too?" The thought of Butch potentially telling me he can't sets me into a sudden panic. "I can't leave him, Butch. He's diabetic and a diva. He needs me. He—"

Butch stops me before I can rattle off all the reasons why I need my food-obsessed, klepto of a sausage to be with me wherever I go. He chuckles. "A diva?"

Frankie wiggles around in Butch's lap, turning toward the steering wheel and putting his front paws on the center so he can gaze out the windshield.

"Yes." I laugh, distracted as I quickly snap a few pictures. "Oh my god, Frankie. Look at you driving a big truck."

Butch slows, having to hold Frankie's chest as he takes the next right. I take a short video to send to Alison as we head up the road another few miles before finally turning down a gravel drive. *We're here.*

The driveway is practically invisible—no mailbox, no reflectors, no signs of residence beyond this point. We head straight through the trees around a slight curve upward as it opens to the cleared landscape.

I hold back a gasp from the most beautiful, picturesque hillside log cabin I've ever seen. *He built this*, I remember the comment Janice made not too long ago.

The stunning two-story cabin is lined with tall bay windows, a large cobblestone chimney, and an amazing overhang porch—to name a few—all overlooking the town in the valley and distant mountains. Even seeing it from where I'm sitting in the truck is giving me chills. I can't imagine the view on that porch at night when the sky is clear and all the stars are shining bright.

Butch parks the truck out front of the massive, two-bay garage that has a similar tone to the cabin. When he opens his door, I say, "Is he okay to wander, or should I put the leash on him?"

"He won't run, will he?" he asks, getting out and holding Frankie in his arms.

I have to laugh at that. "No."

He sets him down as I gather my things and slide out. Butch comes around to my side, immediately trying to take things from my hands.

"I've got this here." Holding my purse and bag, I tip my head to the backseat. "If you don't mind grabbing my safe and...is it okay if we bring the shotgun inside? It's not loaded. I'm not even sure it shoots anymore," I admit.

He takes the shotgun in his hands and examines it carefully. "Where did you get this?"

"It was my great grandfather's," I say. "He passed it down to my grandfather, who passed it down to my father, and well, it's supposed to go to Garrett, but I don't trust him not to...you know, sell it." I'd love to believe my brother wouldn't do such a thing, but after the comments he's made recently...I didn't want to leave it and find out later how wrong I was.

"You do know what this is, don't you?"

"You mean, do I know you're holding a handmade Italian Beretta SL3 12-gauge," I muse. Some families pass down land or property or even jewelry they wish to span future generations, but not my family. This is probably one of the more redneck traditions you'll find here in Montana. "Yes, why?"

"This is like the Lamborghini of shotguns." His eyes dance over the gun with appreciation for the artifact that it is, and perhaps a bit of jealousy. "Damn. It even has the steel engraving of the game scene." He finally looks up at me as he closes the truck door. "Where the hell did you keep this at the trailer?"

"My closet," I say slowly, raising a brow. "Are you going to steal my shotgun like how Frankie steals food?"

He laughs heartily. "No, but if you'll let me, I'd love to clean it up for you. I've got a temperature-controlled gun safe, too, we can keep it in."

I smile. "That'd be great. I used to take it down to Jerry at the gun shop in town to clean it for me, but I haven't in a while."

"Not a problem," he replies as I follow him up to the house. "Fuckin' Jerry. I've been talkin' to him about finding me one for—I can't even tell you how long. He never told me he knew someone who had one."

Butch unlocks the side door and pushes in, holding the door for me with Frankie waddling alongside. "Are you some kind of shotgun aficionado?" I ask, kicking off my shoes in the tight mud room space.

Butch does the same. "I've got a small collection of historic rifles and shotguns." He shrugs as if the fact he's a bit of a history nerd isn't a big deal. "Nothing crazy. Just what I like."

I take a mental note of the little unknown piece of him he just gave me to bring up later and follow his lead. Walking further into Butch's house, I'm stunned into silence. *It's beautiful.*

Rustic country décor fills the space. A large open floor plan extends from the grand kitchen to the dining and into the living room where there's a fireplace to match the cobblestone chimney with a huge flatscreen TV hung above it, surrounded by dark leather furniture. All are overlooked by an above balcony with a wood banister and staircase off to the left-hand side. Everything matches in a slew of warm tone woods, hardwood floors extended throughout.

We move through the kitchen, which sits right off the mud room. Floor-to-ceiling cabinetry, granite counters, stainless steel appliances, and a huge center island fitting five stools greet my wide eyes. All facing an orgasm-giving gas stove that I'm itching to cook on.

He sets my stuff down on the island, so I do the same. "Your house is beautiful."

He simply grunts his reply, in typical Butch fashion. "Help yourself to anything in the fridge and pantry. I don't have much, skipped on groceries this past weekend due to work."

I nod and follow along as Butch starts the full tour of the house.

Three bedrooms, two bathrooms, a clear set up of a mancave in the basement equipped with recliners, a pool table, a flatscreen, and a bar. All the bedrooms are on the second floor, the master connected to a spacious ensuite, while the secondary bath is located downstairs. Pushing into one of the two guest rooms, he says, "This'll be yours." He steps to the side for me.

The room is basic. A simple queen-sized bed centered against the far wall with a single nightstand next to the bed with nothing on it.

There are no sheets, no pillows, and only a shallow closet set into the wall with a set of old boots sitting on the floor. Frankie hobbles in, huffing from having to take so many stairs to get up here. I wander around the space a bit, then sit down on the edge of the soft bed.

"The bed is new. Duke has only used it once when he crashed here. I'll get you some sheets," he says, leaving to go down the hall. I hear him open and close a few doors before coming back with a set of beige sheets, a navy blue comforter with tan floral designs on it, and an already covered pillow in a dark grey pillowcase.

He takes a moment to help me make the bed. And when I grab the pillow, an overwhelming scent envelops me—musty sweat mixed with a familiar cologne. I can't help but bring it to my face to smell it in confirmation.

This is...his.

Butch clears his throat as I stare at the pillow strangely. "Yeah, it's one of mine. I thought I had extras, but I don't. I can pick you up a new one on the way back tonight if you don't want to—"

"It's fine," I say, hugging the pillow to my chest and sitting on the edge of the now freshly made bed. A sudden wave of exhaustion hits me and I melt against the comfort surrounding me. "Where are you going?"

"I figured I'd go pick us up something to eat in town and bring it back," he tells me, pausing before asking, "Unless...you want to go out to dinner?"

I hug the pillow tighter. I was so wrapped up in the idea of getting the heck out of the trailer with Butch and away from my brother, I didn't really think ahead. "I have work at the coffee shop first thing in the morning and I don't have my car," I say more to myself than him as I bite my lower lip and think. "I didn't bring any clothes to go out other than something for tomorrow. Shoot. I didn't even grab my dang toothbrush," I groan, burying my face into the pillow.

"I'll take you to work in the morning on my way in. And I've got an extra toothbrush you can have," he says reasonably. I gape up at him scrolling through his phone. Does he always have everything figured out like this all the time? "Where do you want food from?"

"I'm not—"

"You're eating." The grit in his tone leaves no room for discussion. "Do you like Chinese takeout?"

I scrunch my nose. "Too much salt. It makes me bloated."

"All right," he drawls. "Pizza and wings?"

"Eh...I'm not really feeling pizza."

"Fish fry?"

"Meh."

"Subs?"

"I had a sandwich for lunch."

Butch rattles off just about every place in town to get food from trying to appease me—even the grocery store—before he finally huffs out a long breath and decides for us both. "How 'bout we do the Tavern? They've got a full menu. You can pick whatever you want," he says, handing me his phone with their menu pulled up on the screen.

I hum, trying to decide what sounds good when Butch chuckles deeply. I glance up at him watching me. "What?"

His grin is wide and infectious. "Nothing." He tilts his chin to the phone in my hand. "Find anything you like?"

I shrug and hand him back the phone. "My usual is fine. The cheeseburger quesadilla with extra pickles on the side, please."

"You got it," he says, pocketing the phone. "Do you need anything else?"

I look around. "Maybe just where the laundry is?"

"Downstairs in the bathroom. If you open the double closet doors, it's in there."

"Do you have anything that needs to be done?" Gesturing down at my clothes. "I don't want to waste a load on just this."

"You don't have to—"

"I'll go snooping if you don't just show me where you put your dirty clothes, Butch."

He shoots me a scowl. "Snoop all you want. You don't need to be doing my laundry."

I roll my eyes, exhaustion from not sleeping a wink in the last thirty-six hours starting to set in. "Whatever, Butch, I'm too tired to argue with you right now."

He crosses his thick arms over his broad chest, watching me regard Frankie sitting on my feet yawning. "The tall basket in my room," he grunts, and I bite my lip to keep from teasing him. "You can use my bathroom if you want so you don't have to go downstairs."

"Okay." I sigh, feeling slightly emotional over being in this big house alone with Frankie. Even though I know he's just running out to get dinner for us. "Thank you for letting me stay here—well, us." I smile as Frankie lays down to cover my feet fully with his girth.

Butch nods, watching us for a long moment. "Call me if you need anything. I'll be back in an hour."

"We'll be here," I tell him, and the corner of his lip curls as he turns, leaving Frankie and me alone.

Flopping back on the bed, Frankie whimpers to finally be let up so I lean down and hoist him up. He picks a spot, claims it, and closes his eyes to get some much-needed sleep.

I hear ya buddy.

I make quick work of bringing up all my stuff for...the next few days, I suppose. Putting the few things I have away, I push my safe in the closet and use a few hangers to hang up the wrinkled work shirts I grabbed, before heading into Butch's room across the hall.

I linger in the space, surveying my surroundings. The large, unmade king-sized bed now missing a pillow, how he clearly sleeps on the left side—closest to the door, which I like far more than I care to admit—and the lack of décor in here aside from a family photo sitting atop his dresser.

I study the photo for a moment, noting the Easter holiday attire and lack of a smile on a certain grumpy mountain man's face. Even without the beaming smile like the rest of his family, I can tell he's happy. His arms are thrown over his brothers' shoulders and there's a smile in his eyes that can't be denied.

A pang of jealousy hits me over the family pictured in front of me. I had that, too, once upon a time. And I miss it more than ever tonight...and every other night I've been alone.

In an attempt to avoid crying for the umpteenth time this evening, I walk into the attached master bathroom and start the shower. After taking a quick shower, I change into pajama shorts and a tank top before tossing a *full* load of Butch's laundry in the wash with my few items.

By the time I'm done, I'm dragging my feet to my designated room to close the curtains. I flop down beside Frankie sleeping—who hasn't moved one chubby muscle—on the bed. "Five minutes," I yawn as he wiggles closer to me for warmth and

I double-check my alarms—yes, plural—for work in the morning. "A quick cat nap and I'll be good to go."

I bring Butch's pillow closer and relish in the scent still on it and now on my skin after having used the two wash products he owns.

I absently wonder what he would think of my six products to his two. The image of his scowling face telling me it's a waste of money lures me to sleep. And when he wakes me up to eat an hour later, I ask him. And I laugh until there are tears in my eyes when he tells me I must be dreaming because, *"No one uses that many products to take a damn shower."*

Thirteen.

Butch

"We're takin' bets here, boys," Stan announces with a chuckle. "Tanner, what're ya in for?"

"Twenty says three days max." Tanner smirks.

"All right, I got fifty she stays through the week and into next," Stan says.

Duke snorts. "No way. She's gone by Sunday."

Stan shakes his head with a laugh. "I'm tellin' ya, Butch is gonna be on his best behavior."

I snarl, "Are you assholes done?"

"Why? You in a hurry to be somewhere?" Duke grins.

I scoff, tossing my hard hat in the truck and checking my phone to see if she's texted or called.

"That's a *hell yeah* if I ever seen one."

"Ya know, that's probably the hundredth time he's checked his phone in the last hour," Stan tells Duke, and I scowl.

"No shit," he mocks. "When you told me I had to get up here to hear this, I thought you were pullin' my leg."

"Did you ever ask her how she installed that hot water tank by herself?" Tanner asks, rubbing the back of his neck.

I cock a half grin. "Why? You need her help putting in yours?"

Tanner's face heats, and we all boom with laughter. He waves us off with a huff in frustration. "Fuck you guys. I'll see y'all Monday." After a quick goodbye, Stan and Tanner head off for the day.

Pains in my ass is what these bastards are.

I open my truck door to get in when Duke asks me, "How's it feel?"

My brow furrows as I turn to him.

"Don't give me that look. I asked you, how does it feel? Going home to someone for the first time. Knowing she's sitting there waiting for you."

I lean against my truck. "Don't know yet," I lie, knowing damn well it feels too good to be true. To the point I'm itching to get home and make sure she *is* there waiting for me.

The repeat vision I've had all day since I took her in to work this morning plays once again in my mind. The one of me getting home and barely getting the door open before she races across the room, calling out to me as she leaps into my arms. It's a lame thought—not even sexual in any way—yet it hits deep all the same.

My brother crosses his arms over his chest. "You're a shit liar." He chuckles. "Don't screw it up, and you never know, tonight might be the first real night in a permanent stay. If you're lucky."

I huff, pushing off the running board and getting inside. When I close the door, I roll my window down. "You already know it feels good," I tell him. "You should try finding it again for yourself sometime."

Duke sighs heavily with a shake of his head before he turns away, stalking over to his company truck.

Duke lost his wife, Rachel, to a four-seater plane crash, nearly five years ago. The plane lost all engine control, took a nosedive, and all passengers died on impact. It was a rough time for our family, but even rougher for my brother. None of us knew it at the time, but Rachel was six weeks pregnant. They hadn't even gone to the first appointment yet. Duke lost not only his high school sweetheart but his future child that day.

He's had a hard time snapping back from it. He's been on dates, but nothing ever lasts past the second or third date. He just can't see himself with anyone else—or so he's told me on a few drunken benders.

I don't blame him; I had the same feeling when Cassidy came back to town three years ago. And I get that's why he's been pushing me so hard after finding out about my feelings for her.

You could say seeing her smile each morning was enough for me to even entertain the idea of putting myself back out there like that. Back to a place like I was in with Mary—thinking of marriage and kids—before the bitch cheated on me. It only took me two years of self-loathing, and another three to even dream of getting to this point with Cassidy. But five years later, after the heartbreak that shaped me into an even bigger asshole, here we are.

So, as I pull into my long drive at an early 5:45 PM, I can't help but grin when I spot her Jeep parked in my usual spot. She texted me earlier, letting me know Alison was going to take her back to the trailer to get her car and more of her belongings. I told her to wait, that I'd take her in case her brother had anything smart to say about it, but she said it was fine.

I'm still not happy she went without me, but what can I say? She hasn't messaged me otherwise since then, so yeah, as Stan commented earlier, I've been checking my phone a bit more than usual. Worried about her and how everything went.

Parking beside her car, I get out and make my way up to the side door. When I open it, I'm immediately hit with the most mouth-watering aroma of a home-cooked meal.

Frankie yips, and I hear his nails click on the hardwood as he waddles over to greet me.

"Butch?" Cassidy calls, and my heart swells in my chest hearing her call out my name like that. Is she happy I'm home? Did she miss me?

I shake off the last thought as useless butterflies begin to flutter in my stupid gut. "Yeah," I holler back, kicking off my boots at the door.

I head straight into the kitchen—dying to know what she cooked that smells so damn good. Frankie comes over to where I'm standing, no doubt searching for his plate of whatever it is. Cassidy appears from the living room where she's got a basket of clothes half folded out on the couch. She's wearing jogger sweats and a tank—no bra, I note—with hair tossed up in another pile on top of her head, makeup-free and still refreshed from finally getting the rest she desperately needed last night.

"Hey, how was your day?" she asks, moving to the stove where a pot full of cooking pasta sits with a casserole dish filled with chicken parmesan on the counter beside it—sauced and cheesed up, ready to eat.

"Good," I reply. "You went shopping?" I didn't have chicken here when I left this morning, let alone whatever fancy-looking pasta she's got in this pot.

"Oh, yeah, you weren't kidding when you said you didn't have much," she teases, stirring the pasta. "I don't know of any recipes you can make with just beer and corn chips."

I scratch my bearded chin. "Yeah, sorry."

"Dinner should be done in a few minutes if you want to clean up, or whatever you do when you get home."

I gesture to the stairs. "Just a quick shower and I'll be down."

"Okay." Her stunning eyes lock with mine as she looks up at me sweetly. A slow grin splits my face and I force myself to turn away, my heart hammering in my chest.

I try to shake off all these damn *feelings* she's forcing me to feel for her as I make my way up the stairs and into my room. *Mary never looked at me like that*, I subconsciously think to myself. It's hard to say if the thought is helpful or not at the rate this is going.

I close the door, stripping down and tossing my dirty clothes in the now empty hamper. I noticed it last night, scolding myself for letting her bother with it and then praying she didn't gag from the smell coming off my work socks in the process.

In the bathroom, I turn on the shower as a few things catch my eye. Several things, in fact.

All her stuff, sitting right beside mine.

I pause, taking a moment to look around. Her toothbrush next to mine, her body wash next to mine—along with five other shower products I have no idea the use of. A purple shaver and some weirdly named soap that talks about PH balance with flowers all over it. She wasn't joking last night about her excessive number of shower products.

The sink has a small teal toiletry bag off to the side and—being the nosey fucker I am—I open it. It's filled with makeup. I find myself opening every drawer and closet, peering in and seeing what else she's got. When I notice an opened box of tampons under the sink, I chuckle to myself.

I laugh because a box of tampons under my sink is something I never thought I'd feel so damn good about seeing. Hell, everything in here is making me far too happy right now.

What the hell is wrong with me?

I'm in over my head with this woman.

After a quick shower, I put on a pair of dark grey sweats and leave my chest bare like usual. Heading back downstairs, I pull out my phone to texts from Stan and Duke already asking how it's going.

Stan: *Well? Did you ruin it yet, or are you already getting a taste of her?*

Duke: *How's it going over there, bro?*

Me: *She made dinner.*

Stan: *Not the taste I was thinking, but still good.*

Duke: *Nice.*

"Do you normally eat at the island or the table?" Cassidy asks with her back to me as she makes up two plates for us.

"Wherever you want is fine," I say, going to the fridge and grabbing a beer.

She turns to me. "I—" She stops dead, staring at me with a clear, readable expression as I crack open a beer and take a swig.

It's a look she's given me a few times in the last week when I helped her out around the trailer. And I consciously flex at her obvious stare. "You what?"

"I what?" she questions automatically, a hitch in her breath.

I cock a half grin. "You were going to say something."

Cassidy turns away quickly, clearly flustered. She's cute when she's like this. And I find myself wondering what else I can do or say to get her whole body blushing with this delicious flush on her face right now.

"We can eat here."

"What do you want to drink?" I ask as she takes the plates and positions them on the kitchen island. At first, she sets them next to each other, but then she moves one so it's a stool away.

I fight back a burst of laughter as I say, "I can put a shirt on if it's bothering you."

She shakes her head with a laugh. "You're such an ass." She pushes the plates back beside one another. "There's a bottle of wine I bought, it's in the door of the fridge."

I get the wine and set it out, watching with amusement as she reaches up high for the wine glasses I've never used sitting on the very top shelf. Getting on the tips of her toes, she stretches her body as far as it'll go in an attempt to reach them.

I come up behind her, pressing my chest into her back as I reach over her head and grab one for her with ease. "There's a stool in the laundry if you need it," I can't help but comment.

She spins around, pinned between me and the counter now at her back. "I don't need a stool," she mutters, snatching the glass from my hand with a glare as she slips away from me.

"You sure 'bout that?" I smirk, finally taking a seat.

Cassidy rolls her beautiful eyes with a smile playing on those luscious lips of hers. She opens the wine and pours herself half a glass, putting the rest away and coming to sit beside me. We start to eat with Frankie at our feet, dying to catch anything that falls.

"How much did you spend today on food?" I ask, shoveling in a forkful of the best chicken parmesan I've had in my life. Cassidy shrugs, ignoring me and taking a bite of her own. "Cassidy."

She sighs, swallowing before she responds, "I didn't buy much. Enough for dinner tonight and breakfast through the weekend."

"How much?"

"I'd have to look at the receipt. I had to get a few other things," she tells me. "I'm sure you saw some of it. Is it okay that I left everything in your bathroom? I can move it if—"

"No." The very thought of her moving any of it puts me on edge. "Leave it. It's fine."

We continue eating, and I finish long before she does. "There's more if you want me to get it for you," she says.

"How much left is there?" I ask.

"Well, when I cook, I make enough to take for lunch the next day. So, I just doubled that. Do you pack a lunch or...?"

"I buy," I grunt. "Stan usually grabs me something from wherever he's buying for the day. But I'll definitely start taking leftovers if you got any. This was great, Cass. Seriously, thank you for cooking."

Her smile is radiant. "I'm glad you liked it."

Frankie starts to whimper on the floor, and Cassidy turns her attention to him begging at our feet. "Hey, I know you said you normally leave Frankie out when it's nice, but I wouldn't do that out here. I'd hate for something to get him," I tell her, since she decided to leave him inside this morning with my approval. The poor guy was exhausted.

Her eyes go wide. "Like what?"

I shrug, swigging my beer. "Hawk, bear, coyote, wolves. Ma claims she saw a bobcat a few weeks ago, but Dad said it looked more like a large house cat."

"Stop it," she gasps, looking down at Frankie. "We've never had a problem in the trailer park. They must not come into town. Have you ever seen one out here?"

"Oh, yeah, and no offense to Frankie." I chuckle, glancing down at him. "But he's an easy catch for any predator."

Frankie huffs, and I swear he's glaring at me.

"Well, now that you just freaked me out. Looks like we won't be going on our after-dinner walk, Frankie," Cassidy says, grabbing our empty plates and taking them over to the sink.

I raise a brow. "Where were you planning on walking?"

"Up and down the driveway a few times," she says. "We used to go around the park at least once, the big loop was a mile, the small loop was a half mile."

I nod. "Driveway is about an eighth of a mile one way."

"Ooo, you hear that, Frankie." She snickers. "And since Butch has now scared me into not wanting to walk alone with you looking like a snack. Would you mind joining us for our walkies?"

I laugh heartily, loving the smile this woman is giving me. "Yeah, I'll walk with ya."

I help Cassidy clean up and load the dishwasher. She goes through the motions of giving Frankie his small cup of food and medications. He's quick to eat his food—practically inhaling it.

Cassidy heads upstairs, coming back down with a pair of black flip-flops, I slip on my gym sneakers and pull over a T-shirt.

Outside, Cassidy holds Frankie's leash as we start our walk right around sunset. "So, how'd it go when you picked up your car today?" I ask.

"Fine, I guess." She shrugs. "At first, I didn't think he was home, but Alison checked his room and he was in there—passed out cold with a trash can next to the bed. She said he looked awful, but I guess that isn't surprising."

"You didn't talk to him?"

She shakes her head. "No. I just wanted to get out of there without any drama."

I nod, glad she didn't have to deal with any bullshit without me at her side. She's done that for long enough.

"I put a few feelers out there," she says so quietly I almost miss it.

"For what?"

We pause the walk for Frankie to sniff at a tall pine. "If there are any apartments available," she tells me, and my chest tightens. "There's nothing, though. I mean, I had a feeling it might be hard to find something, but...there's nothing, Butch. Whitetail is getting flooded with seasonal tourists almost year-round now. Don't get me wrong, it's great for local businesses, but rentals are going short-term or putting themselves on the Bed and Breakfast listings. And I can't afford to buy in this market." She looks like she's on the verge of tears, sighing heavily. "It's just a lot right now."

She's right. Whitetail's been teaming with tourists the last few years since the new ski resort opened on the mountain. In the summer and fall, people come for the lakeside camping and the hiking trails. When the snow falls, they fly in for the five-star resort. And year-round, they all come for the views and small-town charm.

"You know you can stay here as long as you need. I'm not putting a deadline on you being here," I tell her, because demanding she stays here with me forever isn't an option—yet.

Or is it?

Cassidy gazes up at me with a small smile. "I used to think you were the biggest asshole."

I grin. "I still am."

"Oh, I know," she giggles. "But I'm sorry I didn't try to get to know you before."

My heart swells as I fight the urge to reach out and haul her against me at this moment. "Don't sweat it, I've been told my personality is a sort of barbed wire and electric fencing situation."

She throws her head back with a beautiful laugh. "Does that mean you've got a softer center beneath all the rough exterior?"

I snort. "Nah, just more bullshit."

Cassidy pushes me playfully. "I won't tell, I promise."

I grin wider. "Good. Can't have everyone in town thinkin' they can take their shot at me if they find out I've got a soft spot for fat wiener dogs."

She gasps. "I knew it was about Frankie!"

I boom with laughter as her stunning ocean eyes smile up at me. We watch each other for a long moment, studying one another. And I wonder if this is my chance to tell her how I feel. Too soon? Maybe. But the desire is there nonetheless.

Frankie starts to huff, plopping on his fat ass and panting heavily. We both look down at him with a laugh. Cassidy bends to pick him up, but I stop her. "I'll get him." Bending down, I hoist him up to walk the remaining half of the driveway back up to the house. I cradle him in my arms as Frankie gazes up at me like I'm his savior, and I can't help but chuckle.

"He likes you," Cassidy tells me with a smile.

"Yeah, well, I did drop a noodle earlier. Fucker caught it mid-air," I say, walking behind her into the house. I set Frankie down in the kitchen, watching as he waddles over to his water dish to get a drink.

"So, how do you normally spend your Friday nights?" she asks, following me into the living room as I plop down on the couch beside the remaining unfolded laundry.

"Watch TV, drink a few beers, pass the fuck out." I take a towel and start to fold it. "What about you?"

Cassidy sits at the other end of the couch, folding as well. "Usually nothing if I've got work the next day."

"You work tomorrow?"

She nods. "I've got inventory to do first thing in the morning. Shouldn't be longer than a half day..." We start to talk more in-depth about our regular schedules and routines. She raises a brow at me. "Why do you get up that early if you don't need to be at work until six-thirty?"

"I've got a full gym set up in the garage," I say. "I do an hour morning workout, then shower, change, and go."

Cassidy scrunches her nose. "You workout first thing in the morning? Aren't you tired? I can barely function that early, let alone do a full workout."

"I'm more tired when I get home from work," I admit. "I don't do it every day, three to four times a week."

She starts packing all the folded laundry into the basket to take upstairs, and I stare way longer than necessary at the neat piles of panties she's tucking away. The mental image I create in my mind has my cock twitching with awareness at how close she is to me right now. How easy and natural this whole evening has been.

"Is it okay if I use this basket to keep some of my stuff in?" she asks kindly, setting the basket at our feet.

I cough awkwardly, using the movement to adjust myself. Grey sweatpants might not have been the best option. "Yeah, no problem. What, uh—I mean, you have any plans in mind for tomorrow night?"

"No," she says. "Do you?"

"Well, they got the band playing again tomorrow. No special on margaritas, but they're doing something with the shots. Didn't know if you'd want to go," I offer.

Cassidy shrugs, not making eye contact. "I don't know."

My brow furrows, confused. She loves that local band; she told me it's one of her favorites. "Somethin' wrong?"

"No," she says with a sigh.

I look at her suspiciously. "I don't get it. You're sayin' nothing's wrong, but it's pretty damn obvious to me there is."

Cassidy bites her plump lip, finally looking up at me. "It hasn't really worked out the last few times I've gone out, you know? Probably best that I just...don't."

It's a fair point she's making, given the events of the last few weekends, but she doesn't seem happy with it. And if there's one thing I don't like seeing, it's Cass unhappy. "What would you rather do instead? We could—"

"You don't have to waste your Saturday night with me, Butch," she tells me with a shake of her head. "I appreciate you trying to include me, but it's not necessary."

"It is," I snap with an undertone of a growl.

She regards me strangely, tilting her head to the side like she can't quite figure me out.

For all I've been tiptoeing around this woman and how I feel about her for the sake of my own ego and heart, I'm done fucking around. It's now or never. Either she's going to tell me she feels the same or she's going to tell me to fuck off.

"I'm not going anywhere without you," I say with conviction.

Whether it's what I said or how I said it, something changes in her expression. Her body tenses. "Wh—Why?"

If I'm doing this now, I'm doing it my *way.*

I sit up and reach for her, taking her by the hips and bringing her thigh over mine to straddle my lap. Her eyes widen and her pretty lips part in surprise. I keep my hold on her hips, digging my fingers in firmly to her lush curves as she places her hands flat on my chest.

I'm sure to look her dead in those knee-weakening eyes when I confess, "Because, Sunshine, anywhere without you isn't anywhere I want to be."

Fourteen.

Cassidy

WARMTH SPREADS THROUGHOUT MY chest and slides down my torso to settle low in my belly as his words sink in. I press my hands firmly against his hard, muscular pecs in a lame attempt to keep steady without dropping my full weight onto him.

Is this really happening? Am I sitting in Butch Montgomery's lap while he tells me how he...feels about me?

Get it together, Cass, the guy said one *really,* really, *sweet thing to you. Don't go getting all weak in the knees over a few words.*

Yet, goosebumps tingle along my skin as he draws me closer, watching me intently. If he's waiting for me to say something, he's going to need to give me a few minutes here to process. Because I'm stuck on one thing he mentioned in particular...

Sunshine.

I've never been one for nicknames—romantic or otherwise. All anyone's ever called me is Cass or Cassidy. But something about Butch giving me one feels...natural. Right. Even still, I can't help questioning it. "Sunshine, huh?" I tease lightheartedly. "Hate to break it to you, but I haven't been very sunshiney the last few days. And I'm not blonde."

I attempt to slide off of him, but he holds me firm in his lap as he grins slowly, his eyes dancing over me.

"It fits," he declares proudly with no further defining explanation. "And you don't need to be blonde to be the sunshine in someone's life."

I freeze with a breath in my lungs, heavy with the rampage of my rapid-fire thoughts and questions and—What does he mean by that? Is that what he thinks of me? Is he referring to himself?

Am I, his *sunshine?*

"Oh, Butch," I breathe, at a loss for words as I fight back the tears. No one's ever said something so beautiful to me before.

That's two.

He shifts beneath me, spreading his legs wide so I drop down lower between them as he sits up straighter to be face-to-face with me. "I mean it," he whispers, his voice hoarse with emotion—an emotion I had no idea he was capable of. It's in his voice, in his eyes, I can feel it radiating off of him and into me.

He reaches up for the wild hair that's fallen from my messy updo and tucks it gently behind my ear. "I've never felt like this before—with anyone."

And that's three.

I don't give myself a chance to overthink it another second, I throw my arms around his neck and crash my lips to his in a searing kiss.

Firm, strong hands grip my ass and haul me flush against a wide, hard chest. I use my lips to pry his open, sliding my tongue between them and having a taste. He tastes like the rugged outdoors and fresh air and all *man*—and *god* it's so good, I can hardly describe it.

I whimper at the overwhelming mix of sensations going through me. The feeling of him holding me against him, the fervor he's causing to stir within me—*for him.*

I want this man, I realize.

I want Butch Montgomery.

His chest rumbles with a deep groan as he lifts me to adjust himself beneath me before falling back on the wide-base couch. I fall against him, my fingers threading through the thick hair on the back of his head, and as my nails scrape his scalp, I give a gentle tug. His grip on my ass tightens almost painfully as he lets me lean away only to nip at his bottom lip.

"Butch," I breathe.

"Right here, Sunshine," he growls, kissing along my jaw and down my neck.

I moan, tilting my head to give him better access in hopes he'll find the spot that drives me wild. He doesn't disappoint. Zeroing in just below my ear, I grind my hips down against him as he uses his tongue and lips to caress my skin. "*Mmm*, yes, right there..."

His massive hands push beneath the waistband of my sweats to grip my bare ass. I physically shiver when his hot, calloused hands knead against the tender flesh. A strong desire is building within me to feel everything his hands are capable of.

Heat floods between my thighs as he palms my ass roughly. "Fuck, baby," he groans, sounding pained. "You haven't had panties on this entire time?"

I pull away, biting my lower lip as I bear down on the hard length straining beneath me. "Is that okay with you?"

Fire flashes in his dark eyes as he captures my lips once again. Our tongues dance in a crazed frenzy and I moan into the kiss as I feel his hand round my ass to brush thick fingers against my core.

Spread open like I am, straddling him, he toys with the damp lips of my pussy. Teasing my sensitive flesh before applying pressure at the entrance to my body. Not enough to push inside like I desperately need him to, but enough to make me clench from the anticipation and slicken with building desire.

"You have no idea how long I've wanted you like this," he mutters against my neck, laying kiss after kiss. He gently strokes me, toying with the wetness between my thighs and driving me wild as I grind against him.

"You have me now," I say, breathless. Leaning back just enough to look him in the eyes, I add, "What are you going to do about it?"

His responding chuckle is deep and lustful. And when he snatches my waist and lifts me with him, I get the sense I'm playing with fire. He turns until my back hits the couch and he lays me out beneath him. I don't get a chance to miss his heat and reach for him before he's on me. I cling to him, running my hands through his tousled hair as we ravage each other's mouths.

He keeps the majority of his weight on me without it becoming uncomfortable—letting me know he's not going anywhere. And it's exactly what I need. Him. This strong man who cares about me, who wants *me*.

When I start to grind up against him with my hips, asking for more, he shifts his weight to lean on one sturdy forearm. He trails his other hand down the curve of my side, his thumb pressing firmly under my breast and ribcage as he tugs my tank top down until my bare breasts are exposed.

He very clearly approves of my *No Bras After Five* rule, as he dips his head to the left while he palms the right. I squirm, lifting my hips for any added friction to go along with the swirl of his devilish tongue around my pert nipple before giving it a long, hard suck.

"Perfect," he says under his breath as he makes his way lower. Both of his hands meet at either side of my hips before taking my pants and slowly sliding them down and around my ass.

I hesitate for a moment. Are we doing this? "What, um—"

"Have dinner with me tomorrow night," he says, cutting me off. His eyes are on me now—firm and sure, waiting for a reply. "Just you and me."

Is he really asking me out? *Now?* I can't help but laugh. "Are you asking me out on a date *while* you're taking my pants off? Usually, in standard format, a guy waits until *after* a date to take a girl's pants off."

He gives me a lopsided grin filled with all the charm in the world. "I'm not like any guy you've been with, sweetheart."

His words glide over my skin and leave a chill in their wake as he pulls my pants off completely, tossing them aside. I watch as Butch shifts to kneel on the ground beside the couch and pushes my thighs apart with ease. He doesn't give me a chance to feel self-conscious or ask if we can turn the lights off as he grips my inner thighs and spreads me for his hungry gaze.

My chest is heaving with anticipation as he pauses, looking up at me watching him. "If you want me to eat this pretty pussy, Sunshine, you're gonna have to give me an answer."

I exaggerate a roll of my eyes. This man, I swear. "Yes, Butch, I will go out with you tomorrow ni—" My voice breaks off into a gasp as his hot mouth meets my sensitive flesh. His tongue delving into my pussy with fervor.

I throw my head back into the cushions with a loud moan when he circles my clit. Strong hands keep me spread wide as he lavishes me with long, firm strokes. It feels so good my whole body begins to tense as his tongue presses against my entrance. I dart out my hand to grip his hair and keep him right where he is. "Oh, Butch, *yes*—"

"*Mmm*," he growls as he pushes his tongue inside me. I arch my back, a gasping mess when he brings his hand closer to the apex of my thighs and his thumb begins to stroke my throbbing bud.

It takes me a moment to notice the shake of his shoulder now pressed against my thigh. I glance down to see his other hand now grasping at the thick, weeping cock he's pulled out of his sweats.

He's getting off while eating me out.

The sight is so erotic, so hot, that my legs start to tremble as my orgasm bubbles to the surface. The slick of his saliva and my need pools between us as I come undone on his face with a cry of his name.

He groans, continuing to pump his tongue inside me as I come down from my high. I watch as his fist pumps harder, jerking his length and chasing his own release.

The urge to taste him in return is overwhelming. I grip his hair and guide him away from my swollen, wet pussy and sit up. He leans back on his heels, giving me a grumpy look that makes me smile at the wetness coating his beard.

Wordlessly, I drop down to my knees beside the couch in front of him and kiss him. Tasting him now mixed with me has me craving even more of him. I push his hand aside and take over, wrapping my palm around his heated erection.

Butch's cock is everything I could have asked for. It's thick and long and feels heavy in my hand. We moan in each other's mouths as I stroke him before pulling away and getting on all fours.

A breath later, I'm taking him in my mouth. His whole body jerks, hips bucking as I swirl my tongue around the head of his cock.

"Fuck," he hisses. "Sunshine, I'm not..." I moan around his length, taking him deeper as he grabs a fistful of my hair. "...gonna last."

I bob my head up and down, shuttling his cock over my tongue and down my throat until I gag. He guides my head back, letting me have a breath before shoving himself past my kiss-swollen lips. When I bring my hand up to grip the base of his cock tightly, he loses control. Fucking my face, he guides me with his hold still in my hair for a moment until I feel his cock swell in my mouth.

"Tell me where," he grunts, a panting mess, "to come."

I fight back a smile at his words. Worried that I'm one of those girls who hates cum in their mouth. And if I was with anyone else right now, I would be, but with Butch... I *want* to taste *all* of him. I redouble my efforts, showing him where I want him to come apart.

"Oh, fuck, baby..." He's moaning now, his whole body tightening as he releases deep in my throat. My throat works to swallow the salty, masculine taste of him, but there's so much, it spills out the sides of my lips still stuffed with his manhood.

It takes him a moment to regain his composure before he lets go of my hair and I pull away. He's quick to grab a towel from the basket and reach for me as I sit up. When he sits down beside me on the floor, he brings me sideways into his lap while handing me the towel.

"You good, Sunshine?" he asks, his eyes still half-lidded.

I nod, wiping the excess from my lips and chin.

He holds me closer—as close as I can be—and kisses me. With no regard for the fact he just came in my mouth. I relax into the warmth of him, of his skin pressed against mine, and given I'm only wearing a bunched-up tank top around my waist, it's a bit chilly on the floor.

When he finally breaks the kiss, I sigh in contentment. I've never enjoyed kissing someone more in my life. I could kiss him all day and be sated by nightfall. Shifting in his lap, I fix the straps of my tank top back into place and start to say, "We should—"

He cuts me off with a groan, burying his face into my neck and holding me tighter to him. His beard tickles as he lays firm presses of his kiss-swollen lips against my heated skin. I sigh, loving how sure he is in every move he's making. There's a confident desire there now, I realize, and I'm upset with myself it's taken me this long to notice it over the last week—or longer.

"I don't want..." he mumbles while trailing off, not finishing his sentence.

"I'm not going anywhere, Butch," I whisper in his ear before kissing his temple. "I won't change my mind while I grab us dessert, if that's what you're worried about."

He reluctantly pulls away, studying me with a serious expression for a long moment, seemingly lost in his own thoughts. Part of me wants to ease whatever worry is plaguing him, while another is more curious to see what he'll do or say next.

Butch leans in to kiss me deeply. "You sure I can't convince you to let me have *you* again for dessert?"

I suck in a breath and shift in his lap. "I wouldn't want to spoil your appetite."

"Sunshine, you have no idea the hunger I have for you," he says, nipping playfully along my jaw and neck.

I sigh, not only from his words, but how he's proving them even now. "Butch..."

He adjusts me in his arms, lifting me with him as he stands and setting me on my feet. Still pressed against him, I can feel the growing bulge in his pants that commands my undivided attention. I glance down. "Maybe we could—"

"Nope." He grins wickedly, following my line of sight. "If my girl wants her dessert, she'll get her dessert." He leans down, giving me one last kiss before he grabs the basket of clothes he pushed out of our way at some point and thumbs through my stack of folded panties.

My brow furrows. "What are you doing?"

"Getting these," he says, picking out my black seamless thong and handing it to me. "Put 'em on."

I cross my arms over my chest, feeling a bit defensive—but still not looking past his little *my girl* comment. Does he have a problem with me not wearing underwear while lounging around the house? I wear them in public, of course, but sometimes it's nice to let the woman breathe. "Why?"

He chuckles, amused by my question for some reason. "Because, Sunshine, I only caught a glimpse of your sexy ass in these a few weeks ago. And I'd like to enjoy the sight of you walking around my house in them. That all right with you?"

I knew he saw my ass!

I mock-glare at him, trying desperately to stop the smile on my face that's starting to make my cheeks ache. "Fine," I huff, snatching the panties he's chosen and slipping them on. "But I'm picking the movie."

He grins. "Wouldn't have it any other way, sweetheart," he says, kissing me before heading toward the kitchen. "So, what'd you get us for dessert?"

"Cheesecake," I say, following after him. "New York style."

He grins over his shoulder. "My favorite."

"Is it?" I smile, grabbing the cheesecake from the fridge while he gathers us two small plates and utensils. "Good to know."

Butch comes up behind me, wrapping his arms around me as I plate our dessert. He dips his head into the crook of my neck and inhales deeply. "I'm glad you're here."

Something changed between us in the last few hours—the last week, in truth. I've never felt more desired, more cared for by someone. It's a stark difference from the last few years of dealing with the death of my father, my runaway mother, and my spiraling brother. Now, with Butch by my side, holding me how he is now, I feel like we could handle anything. Together.

I set the plates aside and cover the rest of the cheesecake to put away before turning in his arms. I hum, sliding my hands up his bare, chest hair peppered pecs and over his wide, solid shoulders. "Me, too," I whisper, bringing him in for another panty-melting kiss.

Fifteen.

Butch

I WAKE IN THE middle of the night to the woman of my dreams lying sprawled out over me with her head on my chest. My arm cramps and I shift ever so carefully, not wanting to disturb her and ruin the moment.

The clock on the wall tells me it's two in the morning, and with the TV back on the home screen, I gather we fell asleep at some point during the movie. I still can't believe she convinced me to sit through two hours of *The Notebook*. But I had to. The way her eyes lit up when she picked it, it felt like a test. Joke's on her because I enjoyed it for the most part—not that I'll ever admit that to another living soul, mind you.

She'll soon realize I'm in this for her and only her. When it comes to us, she'll have anything her pretty little heart desires without complaint from me.

With that all too pleasing thought in mind, I hold her to my chest as I roll us to lay on our sides with her pinned between myself and the back of the couch. She doesn't fuss, hardly stirring as she lets out a breathy sigh when I draw the throw blanket higher over us.

I'm almost asleep when I hear my phone vibrating loudly with a rattle on the coffee table. I glance back over my shoulder at it lit up and flashing. Who the hell is calling me at this hour?

I debate getting up and answering, but the thought of moving and waking Cassidy is like grit in my eyes. Unfortunately, whoever it is, they're not letting up. *Fuck*. I gingerly pry myself from Cassidy's warm embrace and slide off the couch onto the floor, nearly landing on Frankie sleeping beside us. I make sure she's tucked in, even shifting the pillows around for her so she doesn't miss me too much.

Christ. If any of my brothers saw me right now, they'd laugh their asses off. I'd never live it down. Not that I give a shit. When it comes to my girl, I'll gladly look like a fool for her. Because that's what she is now—*mine*.

I grab my phone off the table and stand. I clean up a bit on my way to the kitchen, picking up our used dishes and whatnot before checking my phone. Two missed calls and a text message, all from an unknown number.

Unknown: *I'd like to take you up on that offer. Call me.*

My brow furrows as I try to figure out who the hell... Then it hits me. There's only one person who could possibly be calling me this late that'd say something like that.

I glance back up toward the couch, my thumb hovering over the call button. Should I wake her up and tell her? I haven't even thought about what would happen if her brother took me up on my offer. Shit. I haven't even *told* Cass I offered to get him some professional help the other day at their trailer.

She's been through enough. And if he's calling me and not her about this, there's a reason.

I grab a work hoodie from the hook in my mud room and slip my sneakers on just as Frankie waddles through the kitchen with clicks of his nails. He pauses, watching me. "Come on," I whisper to him, patting my leg. "If your mom wakes up, you'll be a great excuse for why I'm outside."

He huffs, waddling toward me with a lack of enthusiasm that has me fighting to hold in a laugh. I grab his leash and hook his collar as we make our way outside. I hit the call button on the unknown number and wait for an answer.

A nasty sounding wretch precedes a weak spoken, "Hey."

"This is a one-time offer," I tell him, getting straight to the point as the outdoor motion light comes on, I lead Frankie over to the grass beside the garage. "You fuck it up, there are no second chances."

"I hear ya," he says, sounding pained. "My sister with you?"

"Yeah, she's here."

"I...can't see her," he admits. "If I do, I don't know if I can go through with it."

I nod to myself, even though I know when Cassidy finds out he left without saying goodbye, she's going to be more than upset—she'll be devastated. Thankfully, I'll be there when she does. "She'll understand."

"I won't be able to leave knowing...she's alone."

"She's not alone," I all but snap. "She's with me now. And I'm not going anywhere, Clark."

He chuckles on the other end of the phone. "I figured as much."

"She works tomorrow," I tell him. "I'll make a few calls first thing in the morning. Be ready."

He's silent for a long moment before he mutters, "Tell her I'm sorry."

"You can tell her yourself when you're less of a prick," I reply.

"Yeah, I will," he sighs out with a light laugh. "See you soon, asshole."

We hang up and I push the phone into my pocket. Frankie finishes his late-night business and comes my way, plopping down on his ass as he gives me a look of disappointment. "Don't look at me like that," I grump. "I'll tell her soon. Tomorrow. After dinner...maybe."

Now that I think about it... How am I going to tell her that her brother is leaving and she isn't going to see him—for who knows how long—without it breaking her heart and possibly us when she finds out I made it happen? The better question is, *when* do I tell her all this?

I shake off the plaguing question. "I'm doing the right thing here, Frank," I say out loud and unhelpfully as we head into the house so I can get back to where I want to be—where I *need* to be.

I'll do anything for her. For our future together.

And I'm about to prove just that.

Sixteen.

Cassidy

"So then, we watched *The Notebook* and ate half the cheesecake I bought for us," I say with the biggest smile. "We fell asleep at some point after I put on the second movie—I don't even remember what I picked—and when I woke up, we were still cuddled on the couch together."

Alison's mouth gapes open. "You're kidding. Butch Montgomery watched *The Notebook* with you *willingly?*"

"Yes." I smile, a smile I haven't been able to stop doing.

"Tell me again about how he looks without a shirt on," Janice says, fanning herself. "I need something to think about when I go home to Billy tonight."

I laugh.

"Be honest," Alison whispers. "If he tried to…you know, would you have?"

I bite my lip. I may have left out a *few* minor details for the ladies in my *public coffee shop* version of last night. Would I have had sex with Butch last night if he led our *activities* in that direction? Maybe. But he didn't. He chose to give me a dripping orgasm and ask me out on a date.

And the reminder of our date later tonight has me giddy all over again.

"Honestly, maybe. He was being so sweet, guys, I've never had a man simply *want* to see me happy and just be there for it. Regardless of what we were doing. It was a really good night."

Peggy starts to sniffle, dabbing her eyes with a napkin. "Oh, Peggy, what's the matter?" Janice asks, rubbing her arm soothingly.

She waves us off. "Don't worry about me. Keep going, Cassidy."

I go to her, pulling her in for a hug. "It's reminding you of Joe, isn't it?"

She nods against me, sniffling.

The bell chimes and in walks Wade. When he sees Peggy, he comes right over, like he already knows. Wade and Joe were best friends way back when, and like Peggy, he's a widower as well. He ushers her to join him at his favorite table by the window. They sit, and I gather Wade's usual and a hot tea for Peggy.

Back behind the counter, Alison holds a hand to her chest, whispering quietly to me, "When is she going to see the look in his eye he has for her?"

"I don't know." I sigh, watching Wade clasp Peggy's hands in his from across the table. "I guess sometimes it's hard to see what's right in front of you."

The bell chimes again and I gaze up to Butch's half-cocked grin coming in the door. A beaming smile splits my face instantly at the mere sight of him. I quickly grab the to-go cup I set aside for him where I wrote: *Trust the timing of your life.*

"How was your drive in?" he asks, tossing cash onto the counter.

"Fine," I say, gathering his order. I had planned to make us breakfast this morning as another thank you, but I slept through my first alarm. Must have had something to do with being curled up around a certain mountain man. "Was Frankie okay after I left?"

"Yeah, he sat and watched me take a shower." Butch chuckles. "I wrapped him up and put him on the couch like you said. He was already dozing off when I left."

"Lucky dog," Janice mutters and I bump her with my hip as I pass her.

"Any big plans for the day?" I ask, cashing him out.

"Errands," he grunts, taking his change and tossing it in the tip jar.

"Oh, I meant to ask you, where do you get your mail?"

"I've got a box at the post office here in town," he tells me. "Why? Did you need something sent out?"

"No. I ordered some new graphic pens for my tablet a while back that went on backorder, and I just got the alert they'll be shipping soon," I say. "Would it be okay if I have them sent to you?"

Butch gestures with his phone in hand. "I'll text you the box number."

"Thank you." I'm momentarily surprised when he decides to lean over the counter, eyes alight with mischief. I didn't know we were at the PDA level yet—or what we even are romantically, aside from our date later—but it seems like he's decided for us. I giggle at his obvious goading, getting on my toes to meet his expectant gaze with a peck on the lips.

He grins as I drop down to my feet, my cheeks flushed when I realize everyone in the coffee shop is watching us. "I'll see you later," he says.

I smile. "Can't wait."

His grin widens before finally turning and walking out the door.

Once he's gone, I turn to Alison and Janice staring at me. They share a look, with the same stupid smile on their faces.

I huff in annoyance, already having an idea what they're thinking, but ask anyway, "What?"

"Nothing," Alison says, her voice higher than usual as she pretends to retie her apron. "I just didn't know you two were so...official. Would've been nice to hear that from my best friend before I saw it for myself."

I roll my eyes at her weak attempt to fake her feelings being hurt. "We're not—" Are we? When I think back on the events from last night and how natural everything felt. How comfortable we were together. I suppose from the outside looking in, it would seem that way. "We haven't had that sort of conversation...yet. We're still feeling it out."

Janice snorts. "Feeling what out, exactly? Did you see the look on that boy's face? I have *never* seen him smile like that before. There is no doubt in my mind, dear, that boy is head over boots for you."

"Agreed," Peggy shouts from her spot with Wade. At my wide-eyed glare, they share a laugh, returning to chat amongst themselves.

"He is not." *Is he?*

"We shall see," Janice sings, restocking the cups. "Where's he taking you for dinner tonight?"

I shrug, cashing out another customer. "He didn't say."

"Probably Red's Steakhouse," Alison says. "It's the nicest place in town. Did you know they made it so you need reservations Thursday through Sunday now? All this tourist traffic from the resort has been wild for business."

"That it has," Peggy comments on her way behind the counter, seeming to be in better spirits after her conversation with Wade. "Cassidy, can I see you in my office for a moment, please? Janice, take over at the register for a bit, will you?"

"Sure thing, ma'am." Janice salutes, taking my regular place at the register as I turn to follow Peggy through the kitchen to her office in the back.

She pushes her way through the flimsy wood door and into the organized clutter she's deemed her office. The space is so small, I'm pretty sure it was originally meant to be an employee closet.

Peggy plops down in her worn-out desk chair and swivels toward the filing cabinet.

I grab the metal folding chair off to the side and open it beside her. "Did you need help with the books again, Peg? I told you I handled inventory earlier; I'll get it logged in for you before I leave for the day."

Over the last few years, Peggy's been putting my business degree to use. Having me help her with the books, inventory, payables, receivables, and payroll—it tends to be a lot for her to handle on her own, so I try to help as much as I can with whatever I can.

Which tends to be a lot and with just about everything.

She waves her hand absently. "No, no. This is for something else." I watch her flick through several drawers, muttering to herself before she finally finds what she's looking for. "Here we are." She turns her chair to face me, handing me a manila folder. I take it from her as she starts to explain, "A few weeks ago, I was approached by a woman who works for Winton's Resort. She asked me if I'd be willing to franchise Cup O' Joe so they can put one inside the resort itself. That way people don't have to come down the mountain and into town for a taste of our *small-town charm*. Or so they claim."

My eyes widen. "Franchise Cup O' Joe? Oh, my—Peggy, that's amazing!"

"Is it?" she huffs, flustered as she leans against the back of her chair. "I can barely keep up here most days. I don't know if I could handle a second location."

Now it's my turn to wave *her* off. "Oh, stop that. You know I'll help you. It's nothing but a few extra numbers when you get into the swing of things. You already have all the contacts, and we talked about hiring a few more part-timers to cover weekends and early mornings with Alison in the kitchen." I flip open the folder, scanning what appears to be multiple contracts on the location, pricing approvals, schematics, and lease agreements. "If you're worried about all these fancy words and numbers, I'll look it over for you no problem. You know I wouldn't let you take a deal like this if it wasn't good."

Peggy sighs. "I just... I don't know. I'm having a hard time with the idea someone else would be running a store under our name. And so close by? What if it hurt business here? We've been doing so well the last five years; it's truly been a blessing."

I can tell this has been weighing heavy on her mind. She throws her worries and fears out in the open, and I nod, listening as I skim some of the fine print on the contracts.

"They seem very adamant about it being Cup O' Joe. Not one of those fancy, nationwide chain coffee houses," she tells me. "They want *us*. It's quite flattering, now that I think about it."

"It is." I smile, setting the folder on the desk. "But you don't have to franchise to get a location at the resort."

Peggy blinks at me, confused. "They said—"

"There's paperwork and contracts in there not only for a possible franchise partnership but for *you* to *lease* the space, Peggy. You could just open another location. It would be yours. You wouldn't have to deal with some stranger trying to change things or make decisions without your approval."

"Hmm," she hums to herself, thinking. I give her a moment to process like I usually do when we've discussed changing vendors or ordering new appliances rather than opting for continuous repairs.

She sits up, leveling me with a serious expression. "I've had close to three weeks to think about what I wanted for the future of Cup O' Joe, and every time, I come back to the same conclusion."

"And what's that?"

"I need a partner."

I have to agree with her. "That would make your life a lot easier. Especially if you plan on moving forward with opening another location. Have you talked to Lindsey?" Lindsey is Peggy's daughter and only child. She's married with three babies of her own, but she's never shown much interest in the coffee shop.

"I have." Peggy shakes her head. "She already owns ten percent of the business. A silent partner, I believe they call it. I only did it because if anything were to happen to me—"

"Don't even talk like that," I say, cutting her off. "You've got decades left ahead of you."

She chuckles. "I sure hope so, but still. It was a good backup plan, or so I thought. I spoke to her about this a few days ago. And unfortunately, she wants nothing to do with it. She simply said I have her full support on whatever I decide to do."

"Oh." I guess that's fair, given she and her husband are trying for another baby. She wants to focus on her family, and there's nothing wrong with that.

"Wade thinks I should sell and buy a vacation house in the Keys," she adds, laughing. "I'm sure he was just joking, but I wouldn't doubt he'd like to go out of state fishing for those tropical bass he reads about."

I giggle. "I bet."

"What do you think I should do?"

I shrug. "I think getting a partner is a great idea. And probably the only option if you still want to take this deal without franchising out. Or, you could tell them no and keep going how you have been."

"Well, I don't think saying no is a good idea. They'll put one of those overpriced, bland-tasting chains in there and then we'll really be in for it," she says. "No, I think the best option is to have you become my partner and we open the second location of Cup O' Joe together."

I don't know when I started nodding along with her—likely when she mentioned the bland-tasting coffee chains—but I freeze. My mind racing to catch up. I stare at her for so long, tears form in my eyes. "Peggy...you can't be—"

"Oh, I'm very serious, dear." She leans forward, taking my hands in hers. "I have known you your entire life, Cassidy. I have watched you struggle and fight and sacrifice so much for the good of everyone around you." Tears begin to well in her eyes. "You have been nothing short of a daughter to me these last three years, and I can think of no one better for the job."

A small sob escapes me as I lunge forward, engulfing her in a tight squeeze. She hugs me back, her words settling over me.

I've always been grateful for the relationship I've grown into with Peggy. When I came back from college all those years ago to care for my father, I was stressed and heartbroken and dealing with more family issues than any one person should be allowed to take on. Peggy was there for me. And when my mother up and left without so much as a goodbye, she taught me it was okay to let her go.

It was okay to be mad and upset and to grieve her absence.

And I grew to learn on my own it was okay to open her place in my heart for someone who wasn't her. To someone who truly cares and wishes nothing but success and happiness for me.

The thought chokes another sob out of me. I wish my brother could let everything go the same way I have.

We hug for another long moment before we finally part. "All right," Peggy sniffles, grabbing the box of tissues off her desk and handing them to me. "Enough of that. We've got lots to do...*partner.*"

I snort, half sobbing in time with my laughter. "You don't have to make me partner, Peg. You know I'll help you do everything without it," I admit, realizing something else, "I...can't afford to compensate you my share to become a partner."

She scowls at me. "You think I'm worried about money, dear? With everything you've been doing for Cup O' Joe over the years, I probably owe *you* money."

I laugh, shaking my head. "I couldn't possibly—"

"Hush." She pats my leg. "We'll worry about that later. For now, I want you to help walk me through some of these contract terms and agreements. Time to put that fancy state degree to real use."

I smile, wiping my eyes as I clear a space for us. There's a lot to go over and so much to do. A rush of excitement floods me as we start to talk about the expansion and what that'll mean for the business—and for me.

I can't wait to tell Garrett.

I can support us with this. We can find a better place and get out of the trailer park. Out of living alongside all the sad memories and make a change. *This could be exactly what he needs*, I think to myself, giddy at the idea of reconciling with my brother and moving forward.

Then I think of what Butch said, that I need to be patient and wait for him to come around. A wave of emotion sweeps over me thinking about Butch and last night. And our date later this evening.

Everything is falling into place.

A simple saying pops into my head: *Trust the timing of your life.*

Seventeen.

Butch

I LEAVE THE PARKING lot of the coffee shop with the taste of
Cassidy on my lips and a tightness in my heart. I already can't
stand the fact I'm lying to her. Although, I suppose heading to
pick up her brother and take him to rehab *could* be considered
an errand.

Since we woke up late, sleeping through several of Cassidy's
hundred-and-one alarms, she was in a bit of a rush this
morning. Which worked out for me since I had some phone
calls to make the second she was out the door.

I was able to find an opening at a rehab facility west of
Billings that works with alcoholics—two and a half hours away,
mind you. Making a five-hour round-trip drive wasn't exactly
a part of the plan for today, but I have no other option.

There are probably a million other things I could be doing with my Saturday morning, and instead, I'm on my way to Cassidy's old place—because that's what it is now, her *old* place—in Whitetail Park.

I pull off on the side of the narrow street out front. Garrett's shitty, beat-up ranger pick-up is parked exactly where it was last time I was here—the night I took Cass home with me. Hard to believe that was only two days ago. It feels like I've lived with her in my arms forever.

And I fully intend to keep it that way.

Starting with fixing her damn brother.

I leap up the short porch steps and pound a fist on the front door. It shakes under my heavy hand and I have to remind myself to keep my cool. *I'm doing this for my Sunshine, not for him or anyone else.*

The door finally opens and Garrett stands in front of me, disheveled and appearing worse off than when I left him Thursday night. "Hey," he croaks, opening the door fully and stepping aside.

"You ready?" I ask, walking past him into the trailer. I glance around. It's hard to say if he attempted to clean up or if he just kicked shit out of the way. Either way, the place is in shambles. "Would it have killed ya to clean up in here?"

He scoffs, shuffling to the couch and picking up a backpack in one hand and a guitar case in the other. "Honestly, yeah, it would've."

When he turns back to me, I shut my mouth. If I had to guess, he hasn't had a drink since after his big fight with Cass. Or, he drank everything and then decided to cold turkey it afterward. Again, hard to say, but it's probably best I don't ask.

I give a subtle nod for my own sake, dropping the subject. The guy looks like hell, but he's making an effort to change things—that's why I'm here—I need to cut him some slack. "That everything?" I ask, gesturing to his bag and case.

He nods.

"Let's go, then," I say and he follows me out, locking the door behind us.

When we get in the truck, I expect him to talk, maybe ask a few questions about where I'm taking him at the very least. But he doesn't say a word. And we end up making the two-and-a-half-hour ride in silence—aside from the radio going in and out when we cut through the mountains.

When I pull into the long drive of the facility and bring us to the front door, I throw the truck in park and glance over at him for the first time in easily an hour. He's pale. A fine sheen of sweat coating his brow and neck as he gazes out the window.

The building is newer, clean cut and painted a white-grey over the brick. The grounds are spacious and neat with pleasant to-the-eye landscaping. Looking around has a tension easing off my shoulders. I thought I felt good about this before... Now, I feel a hell of a lot better leaving him here for however long it takes to get his head on straight.

I hadn't planned on going in, but the way he's staring out and not moving, I might have to. "You need me to walk you in?" I ask, attempting to break his silent stare.

The double doors to the facility open and two men step out, patiently waiting as well. They knew we'd be coming, and I made the baseline payment to reserve his spot over the phone earlier. This place isn't free. Or cheap.

Garrett takes a deep breath. "I'll be all right," he says, and I'm not sure if he's saying that for my benefit or his own.

Wordlessly, he gets out, grabbing his backpack and guitar case from the backseat. When he closes the door and starts to walk off, I roll the window down. "If you need anything, you call me."

He stops, turning to the side and slinging one strap of his bag over his shoulder. "Yeah, I will."

I'm not great with goodbyes to begin with, and this situation is already tense, so I give him a nod and shift the truck into drive.

"Hey," he shouts before I take my foot off the brake. "You take care of her for me. I'd hate to have to kick your ass after this."

I crack a lopsided grin. "I'd like to see you try."

He grins back, the first real bit of emotion I've seen from him all morning.

"Take care of yourself, brother," I say, finally driving away and spending the entire ride home thinking about my girl and how badly I want to see her.

I step out of my truck, making sure to bring the assorted bouquet of flowers with me that I stopped for on the way home. I don't linger long, striding past Cassidy's Jeep parked beside me as I head up to the house.

I'm late.

We'll still make our dinner reservation on time if we leave soon, but I'm going to have to move my ass if I want to get a quick shower in beforehand. After dropping Garrett off this morning, I drove back to town and headed up to the logging site to do some basic maintenance on a few pieces of equipment, which ended up taking longer than anticipated. On my way home, I passed a truck full of flowers for sale and knew I had to stop. If these flowers cost me smelling like oil and sweat for our date tonight, then so be it.

If they make her smile, it'll be worth it.

Pushing in the front door, I'm met with...silence. I kick off my boots and set the flowers on the island. "Anybody home?" I call out.

"We're up here," her sweet, sweet voice calls back to me and those damn butterflies flop in my gut yet again. Something about her being here, waiting for me when I get home—no matter the time or circumstance—just hits a part of me deep down that I didn't know needed to be filled.

I take the stairs two at a time, stopping at the guest room door, expecting to see her—but she's not there. My brow furrows when I hear a yip from Frankie coming from my room. I walk further down the hall and step inside, the door wide open.

"Hey, you're home." Cassidy smiles at me from her spot perched on my bed. Her smooth, tan legs crossed beneath her with that drawing tablet in her lap. She's clearly ready to go as soon as I am, absolutely stunning in a navy-blue, floral sundress I'm hoping is as short as it looks from here. Her hair is down, cascading in long waves. Everything about her is stunning. She's damn near glowing. "How was your day?"

Frankie wiggles out from beside her, coming to the edge of the bed with a happy tail in greeting as I approach. I give him a rub on the head, right between his ears.

"Good," I say, leaning down to kiss her. She smiles, obliging me with a peck on the lips like she did this morning at the coffee shop. I nearly sigh at the brush of her full lips against mine. I can't help it. This woman brings out the sucker in me. "How was yours?"

"Amazing," she beams. "Peggy asked me to be her partner for Cup O' Joe. We're opening a second location inside Winton's Resort."

Her giddiness has my face splitting in two. "That's awesome, babe. Congratulations."

"I know," she squeals, setting her tablet to the side and climbing up on her knees. "And that's not even the best thing that's happened today."

"Oh, yeah?" My heart thumps in my chest, like the sucker I am. Seeing her happy like this is better than any damn drug out there.

"*Hallmark* bought another one of my cards." She bounces into my arms in her excitement. I scoop her up and hold her tight to my chest as she laughs. Slowly, I slide her down my body, leaning down to hold her as her giggles turn to quiet hiccups.

I lean away slightly, still keeping her close. "Hey now, don't do that," I say, wiping her cheek free of the few tears trailing from her eyes. "What's wrong, Sunshine?"

She shakes her head, clinging to me as she hides her face against my chest. "I'm sorry, it's...nothing."

I turn us until I'm sitting on the edge of the bed, tugging her closer until she's standing between my spread knees. "It's not nothing," I say, smoothing my hands down her arms until I'm gripping her hips to keep her in place. "Talk to me."

She sniffles, dabbing her eyes. "I don't want to make us late and miss our reservation."

"Then we'll go somewhere else," I grunt. "Tell me why you're upset, sweetheart."

On a sigh, she says, "I don't know...it's just...a lot."

I nod, urging her to keep talking.

I'll do anything to get these tears that eat at my soul to dry up.

"Everything feels so right, right now," she whispers, her hands sliding over my shoulders and around my neck. "I'm so happy it's...overwhelming."

"I get that," I say, gently kneading my thumbs into her waist.

Her lip trembles and I tug her closer. "Sorry..." She sniffs, throwing her head back and groaning. "I promise I'm not trying to ruin our night."

"You're here with me, aren't you?" I hum, wrapping an arm around her waist and guiding her into my lap. She hikes her short little number up, swinging her legs over my thighs and straddling my lap. "As long as we're together, nothing can ruin my night."

She smiles, cupping my face in her hands and pressing her mouth to mine in a sensual, slow kiss that has my cock thickening. She pulls away ever so slightly, her lips ghosting over mine with a whisper, "You stink."

I grin, gripping her soft, bare thighs where they meet her ass. I lift her in my arms and turn us, pinning her under me, the mattress now at her back. She gasps at the quick change in position, her arms still locked around my neck as she brings me in for another kiss. She arches against me and I can feel the heat of her body increasing.

My girl likes to get tossed around in the bedroom.

Storing that information for later, I chuckle when her stomach rumbles its grievance against mine. Finally peeling my body from hers, I gaze down at her rumpled dress and pouty lips. "Later," I growl, not able to help myself when I swoop in for one more kiss.

I straighten, forcing my legs in the direction of the shower.

"That better be a promise, mountain man," she teases.

Looking back at her sitting on the bed has me questioning my resolve. I remind myself of her stomach growling against mine a second ago, and the desire to put her needs before mine takes precedence. "I don't say things I don't mean, sweetheart."

After a quick shower, I throw on a clean pair of jeans and a black dress shirt, tucking in the bottom and cuffing the long sleeves mid-forearm. I comb my hair back and spray whatever shit my sister, Lily, bought for me last Christmas over it before heading downstairs.

I arch a brow at the sight of Cassidy wrapping Frankie up on the couch and flicking through channels on the TV. "Ready to go?" I ask, hitting the bottom step and walking toward her.

"Yup, just need to find—" She turns the TV to an old western classic and sets the remote down on the coffee table. "All set."

I gesture between the TV and Frankie's bundled fat ass on the couch. "What's all this?"

"Oh," she giggles. "Frankie's Saturday night westerns."

"His *westerns*?"

I follow behind her as she sways into the kitchen, her waist, hips, and ass begging for my undivided attention. Engrossed in watching her, I almost miss her saying, "He used to sit with my dad every Saturday watching western movies. Even after my dad passed, he watches them every Saturday. He'll cry if I don't put them on for him."

I chuckle. "So, you sit around watching *Butch Cassidy & The Sundance Kid* with Frankie every Saturday?"

She glances up at me, slinging her long purse over her shoulder. "Huh? Butch Cassidy?"

I sit down at one of the kitchen stools to put on my cowboy boots—the cleaner pair reserved for going out. "Yeah, it's an old western movie from the sixties. I probably watched it a hundred times growing up. It's my dad's favorite."

She slips into a pair of sandals. "It...sounds familiar."

"Ah, shit," I mutter before reaching for the door. Instead, I grab the flowers from the counter and turn to Cass, handing them to her. "These are for you."

She giggles, taking them from my extended reach and bringing them to her nose. "I saw. Thank you."

"Yeah, sorry. I fucked that up, didn't I?" I grumble. "Should've given them to you when I got home."

She sets them onto the counter before coming up beside me, slipping her hand in mine with the other holding my forearm close to her. "I love them, Butch. Thank you."

I kiss her again. And again. Because I need to.

She makes everything feel so...easy.

We're in the truck a moment later, heading for town, and crossing my fingers we make our reservation at Red's. I was hesitant about having our first date at the only steakhouse in a forty-mile radius—right in the center of town, no less—but the place is top-notch these days after the resort opened and they took on new ownership. The best damn steak you'll have in Montana is served at Red's. It only seemed right to bring her here.

My girl deserves the best.

"So, have you seen it?" I ask.

"Seen what?"

"The movie you put on for Frank. *Butch Cassidy & The Sundance Kid.*"

"Oh." She shrugs. "I've watched a lot of them over the years. Well, I'd use the term *watched* loosely. I usually have them on in the background for Frankie nowadays."

"Damn. He really is the best dog ever," I chuckle.

She laughs. "You watch westerns, too?"

"Me? Nah. I mean, I'll watch it if there's nothing else on, but it's not a go-to for me."

She hums. "Maybe we'll have to make a date with Frankie next weekend and watch one together—the three of us."

I grin from ear to ear. "Sounds good to me."

When we arrive at the restaurant, the place is packed. Thankfully we're only five minutes late and the hostess takes us right away, seating us by the window with a breathtaking view of the distant mountains that surround our little town.

Cassidy's face lights up at the sight. "Oh, wow, look at that sunset," she says, captivated for a long moment before gracing me with a shy smile. "It never gets old, does it?"

"No," I say, leaning back in my chair and watching her. The way her eyes slowly glide over me and back out the window, the way she rests her elbow on the edge of the tablecloth to peer out with her chin resting on the back of her hand, the deep sigh she exhales that has her luscious breasts rising and falling deliciously in her low cut sundress. "The view from where I'm sitting is better if you ask me."

Her gaze darts to me as a delicate flush rises to her cheeks. "Butch..."

"You look beautiful tonight, Sunshine."

Her smile is radiant. "Thank you. You're rather dashing yourself over there."

Over there... She's got a point.

I stand, taking my chair with me as I move it beside her rather than across from her at our small table for two.

"What was that for?" she asks as I take my seat once again, but the twinkle in her eyes and the smirk on her lips tell me she already knows the answer.

"Getting closer to my favorite view."

She snort-giggles, clamping a hand over her mouth to contain her laughter that only has us both launching into easy, meaningful conversation.

The waitress comes over to take our order, checking in on us periodically throughout dinner when our food finally arrives. We order steaks and a few cocktails—two for her and one for me since I'm driving. We talk about food, life, family. I launch into an in-depth rundown of how my parents met and all my siblings. I pick the cringiest stories to tell her about my brothers from their teenage years to the point I laugh so hard my eyes water and Cass teases me for it.

Last night was the best, lazy stay-at-home evening I've ever had with anyone before. And now, here we are again, having the greatest damn date I've ever been on.

At this rate, I'm in trouble.

She's making it far too easy to fall in love with her.

My stomach, now filled with a great meal, drops. I admit, having my eye on Cassidy for the last three years has caused me to already develop...feelings for her. But to put a label on them—especially one as big as *love*—I have to remind myself it hasn't been long enough for her.

Reeling in my racing heart that wants to leap out of my chest and onto a silver platter so I can hand it over to this incredible woman, I say, "You should come with me to Sunday dinner tomorrow."

Cassidy takes a sip of her drink. "Really? I thought you said it was a family thing?"

"It's mandatory for me and my siblings to be there, according to my mother. But I've brought Stan many times, Lily's brought people, I think Levi's had a few one-night stands join the mix."

She pulls her plump bottom lip between her teeth. "One-night stands, huh?"

"That's not us," I growl, my hand finding her thigh under the table and giving it a firm squeeze. "I—"

"Can I interest you two in any dessert tonight?" the waitress asks, stacking the last few dishes from the table in her hands.

I keep my hand on Cassidy's thigh. "Up to you, babe."

She scrunches her nose, appearing unsure for a brief moment—when a waiter passes by with the dessert tray in hand and her eyes widen.

"We'll take a look," I tell our waitress who excuses herself with a promise to send the tray our way next.

"Aren't you stuffed?" Cass whispers, placing a hand on her belly. "I don't know if I can eat another bite."

I am pretty full. "See what they got. We can always take it home with us."

The dessert tray arrives and I watch my girl peruse her options: tiramisu, crème brûlée, chocolate lava cake, a rich and creamy cheesecake, and an old-fashioned apple cobbler.

She ogles the massive display piece of chocolate lava cake before peering up at me with those deep blue eyes that turn me into a much weaker man. "Will you split it with me?"

I chuckle. Is that even a question? "We'll take the lava cake," I say to the waiter.

"Coming right up, sir."

Her hand finds mine on her thigh, turning it over and threading her fingers between my own. This evening has gone so damn well, I don't think I could've imagined it going any better.

And we haven't even gotten home yet...

I lean in for a kiss at the same time my phone blares to life with an incoming call.

"Goddammit," I curse, fishing my phone from my pocket and flipping it around to see it's Levi calling. What the hell could he possibly want? No doubt Stan told him about my date tonight with Cass. He should know better than to be calling me in the middle of it.

"Answer it," Cassidy says. "I don't mind."

"You sure?"

"It could be something important," she says. "And if it's not, you can tell him to buzz off."

I raise a brow. "Buzz off, huh?"

She rolls her eyes, giggling. "You know what I mean."

I chuckle, swiping my thumb across the screen and bringing it to my ear. "What's up?"

Loud music blasts in the background. "Hey, I know you're busy, but you need to get down here—"

"Who the hell are you calling?" Rhett's voice carries through the phone. "I told you not to call him."

"Too fuckin' late," Levi slurs. "Anyway, you need to come grab Duke, bro. He's all fucked up. Won't listen to anybody. Roger already told him to leave twice. Now he's threatening to call the cops. I'd take him home myself, but Brandy is here and..."

More like *he's* in no condition to be taking anyone anywhere. "What's his problem?"

Levi's quiet for a moment. "You know what day it is, right? Did you forget?"

A wave of guilt slams into me so hard I nearly shout. "Fuck."

"—my name isn't *Brandy*, you idiot."

"It can be for tonight, darlin'." My brother miserably tries to score with some chick while Rhett and Duke shout at one another in the background, but I can't make out what they're saying.

I wave over the waitress to get the check and have dessert wrapped to-go, telling Levi, "We're right around the corner, I'll be there in a few minutes." I hang up the phone, rubbing a hand down my face in frustration. Why didn't he call me? Remind me, even. I could've talked to Cassidy and rescheduled our date.

"What is it?"

"My brother," I say, taking out my wallet and handing my card to the waitress who says she'll be back with the receipt and to-go box. "Duke. It's...the anniversary of his wife's death. Five years ago, today."

"Oh..."

"He's not himself right now," I grunt. "I'm sorry, but I need to go get him and bring him home."

"Of course."

I sign off on the bill and stand, taking Cassidy's hand as she grabs her purse and our dessert. I'm hoping we'll get a chance to enjoy it...depending on what I'll be dealing with tonight. She hurries to keep up with my long strides as we make it to the parking lot and into the truck.

I hit the gas a little harder than I should, guilt clogging up my thoughts. Not only did I forget about today and what it meant for Duke, but I haven't had the chance to tell Cass about her brother yet. And now...I just ended our date early.

Fuck.

Eighteen.

Cassidy

Butch stops the truck right outside the front door to Tavern Nine, throwing it in park. "Wait here," he says, pushing his door open with his boot. He slams the door behind him, eating up the space toward the bouncer and the bar owner, Roger, standing outside as if they were waiting for him.

I nibble anxiously on a fingernail, watching the door as he disappears inside with Roger. I hope his brother's okay. I suppose I'll be finding out soon enough since he'll be getting in the backseat any moment.

Or should I move to the back and let him have the front?

I've known Duke for as long as I've known Butch—years—and I've met him several times and seen him around town on countless occasions. He's the most level-headed, kindest guy I know. The fact that another one of Butch's brothers called *him* to have Duke picked up because he's not himself...well, I can relate to that feeling all too well.

Part of me wonders if Garrett is inside right now, drinking away his sorrows.

I reach for my phone, my chest tight, debating if I should text him to check in or not—while simultaneously trying to decide if I should move to the back seat. The door to the bar slams open and Duke stumbles out with Butch hot on his heels.

"Over here," Butch tells him, trying to scoop an arm under his brother's for support.

Duke jerks away, righting himself. "I know where the fuck I'm goin'."

When he reaches the truck and goes to open the front passenger side door, he looks up. His glossy, heartbroken expression catches mine and he turns away to face Butch. "What the hell, man? I can't—"

"Get in the truck, Duke," he says, opening the back door and tossing a few things out of the way to clear the seat for him. "Now."

"I can get in the back if—" I start to say.

"You're fine where you are, sweetheart," Butch tells me, nudging his brother not so gently in the right direction. "Get. In."

A moment later, Duke is in the back muttering to himself and Butch is shifting the truck out of park and waiting for a car to pass. We pull out onto the road as a retching sound from behind has me spinning in my seat.

"Don't you fuckin' blow chunks in my damn truck," Butch growls.

"I ain't doin' shit." Duke coughs, clearing his throat. "Haven't puked since high school. Relax."

I fish some napkins out of the center console and hand them to the back. "Here." He doesn't bother taking them from my hand or say thank you, so I set them on the back edge of the console. "Just in case."

He grunts.

The cab of the truck falls eerily silent, with nothing but the rumble of the engine and the low hiss of the AC to be heard. Well, this is an awkward way to end a first date.

Butch's hand finds mine resting on the center console. I glance over at him, giving him a small smile as I slide my hand in his.

"Sold the house," Duke grumbles from the backseat.

Butch peers at him through the rearview mirror. "Yeah? That was fast. Didn't you just list it on Monday?"

"Seemed fitting to finally be rid of it after five years."

I cringe a little at the deeper meaning. The very notion he's been holding onto a house he and his wife bought and lived in before she passed...then chose to stay there even after she died... I can't imagine. I give Butch's rough hand a squeeze.

"I was telling Cass earlier about that time Levi got his head stuck in between the stair railing at Ma's," Butch says, trying to lighten the mood. He glances between the rearview and the road. "Remember his face when Ma grabbed the butter and Pops grabbed the chainsaw."

I smile, biting my lip to keep from laughing like we did at the restaurant.

"I should have driven her out to her folks' place like she asked me to." His voice is absolutely broken as he says those heart-wrenching words. Pain and regret radiate from the backseat to the point I'm on the verge of tears on his behalf.

I twist in my seat as Butch says, "Come on, man. Don't go there."

"How could you have possibly known?" I ask. "You can't carry that kind of guilt forever."

Duke's eyes narrow in my direction. "I do know," he says. "She wouldn't have been on Terry Welsh's plane at all had I driven her."

Five years ago...Terry Welsh's plane...I remember that. I was away at college, but I remember the phone call I got from my dad, telling me all about the small plane crash that killed four people due to unforeseen engine failure. The Welshs were close friends of my father's, and I believe Terry was Alison's uncle, but I never asked who else was on the plane.

I remember it being a sad day for our tight-knit community. Things like that don't happen here often, if ever. It was a scary reminder of how fragile life can be.

"You don't know that for certain," I say quietly. "You could've just as well ended up on that plane with her."

Duke's eyes linger on me for a moment, his jaw clenching before he jerks his gaze out the window. Point taken. I slip back into my seat facing forward as we ride the rest of the way to the house in silence.

When Butch parks the truck in his usual spot in the driveway, he climbs out and comes over to my side, taking the to-go container and helping me down. He closes the door and takes my hand, leading us toward the house and leaving Duke still sitting in the backseat with no signs of movement.

I look back over my shoulder. "Shouldn't we help him get inside?"

"He needs a minute to himself," he tells me, unlocking the door and pushing inside. "You hit him with a hard truth, Sunshine. He'll be in when he's ready."

Frankie yips from his spot still parked on the couch. It always takes him a minute to get untangled from his burrito blanket.

Toeing off my sandals, I step into the kitchen as Butch kicks off his boots, following me in. I set my purse on the island, turning around only for him to step closer, pinning me against the counter. His big, mountain-worked hands settle on my hips.

My fingers toy with the buttons on his dress shirt, peering up at him with a bat of my lashes. Not necessarily aiming for subtlety. "Thank you for taking me out tonight. Dinner was amazing."

I expect him to smile, maybe lean in and kiss me, but his expression remains hard. "It didn't exactly end how I thought it would."

I tip my head to the side. "No?"

"Well…" He doesn't get a chance to finish his thought before the front door slams into the wall and chaos ensues.

Duke crashes through the door and trips over my sandals, landing a hard shoulder into the wall as he falls to his knees. Frankie freaks out, likely assuming there's an intruder. Barking and scurrying across the floor, his paws slip and slide over the hardwood, sending him toppling over his own bulk and colliding with one of the bar stools, causing said bar stool to tip over and smack the floor with a loud bang.

"For fuck's sake," Butch mutters as Frankie races around the island to my side in his apparent terror.

I giggle, scooping him up. "Not a very good guard dog, are you, chub?"

"Don't worry about me," Duke grumbles, getting to his feet and kicking shoes out of his way as if they have personally offended him. "I only have to work for a fuckin' livin'."

"What the hell are you going on about?" Butch scowls, attempting to help his brother right himself and getting shoved out of the way.

"Fuck off."

Butch sighs heavily, giving me a stern look that screams *this* is what he was referring to a moment ago. He turns to his brother. "Get your boots off and sit the fuck down," he says. "You're on the couch tonight. I'll be down in a minute, don't say anything that'll get your teeth knocked out."

Duke huffs in response, not bothering to take his boots off, he grabs one of the upright stools and sits down. Butch shakes his head, disappearing upstairs and leaving me alone with a scared sausage dog in my arms and one prickly Montgomery brother.

Setting Frankie down, I get him a treat to help calm him before picking up the stool and putting away the dessert from the restaurant in the fridge. I'm not sure if Butch is feeling up for a movie or not tonight. It's still rather early, not even after ten.

The sound of Duke mumbling behind me has me turning to face him. He appears miserable and disheveled, like he's been carrying this weight on his shoulders all this time and only lets the misery out one night a year. "I'm...sorry," I attempt, choosing my next words carefully. "What I said before, it's none of my business. I didn't mean to overstep or upset you."

Duke's dark eyes lift and he stares at me so deeply I wonder if he even knows I'm here. "I stopped mourning her years ago," he mutters, rubbing a heavy hand over his scruffy chin. "I can go months without thinking about her most of the time, but every day I think..." He swallows hard, tears springing to his eyes, his cheeks flushing. "She was only a few weeks pregnant when she died."

I try to contain my gasp, but I'm unable to halt the spring of emotion that has me bringing a hand to my heart. "Oh, I'm so sorry. I didn't—"

"Not many people know," he admits. "Four, actually. Even after the funeral, I never had the heart to tell her parents that's why she was coming to visit them."

My heart hurts and I clutch the counter in front of me.

"Every day I think about that baby." His voice grates like a dagger—broken and cold. "Every goddamn day. What does that say about me? Mourning the loss of something I never had over someone I had for years."

I...don't even know how to respond. I nod wordlessly, unable to give him comfort in any form. Nothing I say or do for him tonight is going to take away his pain. He may be admitting to me that he's over the loss of his deceased wife, but he's still in mourning—for a completely different reason.

"He loves you, ya know."

It takes me a moment to realize he's speaking to me again and not himself, considering we're the only ones in the room aside from Frankie. I glance at him, slowly letting his words settle in my mind until my heart stops beating. "What, um, makes you say that?"

"He said as much." His head tips from side to side, whether that's him mulling over his thought process that brought him to that conclusion or from being drunk, it's unclear. "More or less."

"Well, which is it?" I blurt, my stomach doing somersaults.

Promise and excitement cascade over me the same way they did when Butch first showed up offering to help me patch the leak in my roof. Duke might not be himself at the moment, but he's one of the few people who is closest to Butch—at least from what I've gathered. If anyone else told me Butch was in love with me, I'd likely disregard them. Right now, however, I can't seem to shake it off as a meaningless statement.

"More or less? What exactly did he—"

"All right." Butch's voice carries down the stairs as he descends. My gaze snaps to him carrying a bundle of blankets, a sheet, and no pillow. "Time for bed, little brother," he says tauntingly, tossing the bundle on the end of the couch.

Duke grumbles something under his breath, pushing off the stool aggressively—to the point I think it might topple over as well. Instead of heading for his brother, he stomps over to the stairs.

Butch scowls. "Where the hell do you think you're going?"

"To bed," Duke huffs, stomping up the stairs one heavy boot at a time.

"You're on the couch," Butch hollers after him, scrubbing a hand down his face when his brother makes no show of stopping. "Goddammit."

I step around the island, pushing the stool back into place. "I can take the couch."

"No." Butch shakes his head, a low growl vibrating his throat as he comes toward me. "It's bad enough you slept there last night."

He tugs me closer to him and I snake my arms around his waist, my chin resting on his chest. Blinking away the emotional roller-coaster of a fragmented conversation I just had with his brother. "So did you. And I can't imagine it was comfortable given your size."

His brow quirks up. "You callin' me fat, Sunshine?"

I snort-giggle and give him a mock squeeze. "You know what I mean."

He huffs, bringing his arms around to fully encase me against his chest and kissing my forehead. "I'll be fine down here if you don't mind sleeping in my bed. Assuming Duke took the spare room and he's not in mine already."

I hum loudly as if to show I'm thinking it over. Although, I think the solution here is fairly obvious. "We slept together last night, we can do it again tonight."

A slow grin splits his face. "Yeah?"

I shrug, trying to tamp down my smile and the butterflies flying south for the evening. "I don't know about you, but I slept pretty good last night."

"I did, too," he says. "Well, maybe a little cramped." He tightens his hold on me. "But I'd do it again with you in a heartbeat."

He loves you, ya know. Duke's five little words repeat in my mind.

I bite my lip. He can keep saying all the nice things he wants; I'll accept them happily. It won't change my mind on where this night is about to lead us.

And I don't think I'd have it any other way.

Nineteen.

Butch

"Did you want to watch a movie or..." I hesitate saying the words *head to bed* out loud. My cock is already stirring with Cassidy pressed against me how she is now. I don't need to set any expectations on her if we decide to call it an early night.

"We can, if you want," she says, her hand caressing low on my back. It feels so damn good I want to flop over on my back the way Frankie does and let her rub me all over.

I am truly gone for this woman, there's no doubt about it.

"Or...we can go upstairs and finish what we started last night," she offers with a smile on her lips and a naughty spark in her eyes. Her soft caress on my back turns to a light dig of her nails as she tugs my shirt up to untuck it.

I grin wide. *Whatever my girl wants.*

I don't hesitate, bending at the knee and scooping her into my arms bridal style. Her laughter urges me on as I head for the stairs, slender arms locking around my neck. I take the stairs carefully two at a time, mindful of the woman clinging to me. Passing the open doorway to the guest room, I'm grateful Duke chose to crash in there rather than my room.

Cass sees him, too. Dirty boots still on, half flopped on the bed at an awkward angle. "Maybe we should—"

I grunt, steering us toward my room and depositing her on the edge of the mattress before I flip the light switch on. The glow from the two bedside lamps illuminates the room with a soft, golden light. And the way she peers up at me—long, dark hair down and brushed to the side, smooth, pale neck tilted back—has me cursing my asshat of a brother tenfold. "Stay here," I say. "I'll get him sorted."

I fight back the urge to stomp my feet down the hall out of sheer aggravation and hurry to yank off my brother's boots and set them aside. I shove his lower half fully on the bed and call it good. Not much else I can do when he's chosen to fall on top of the covers.

Stepping back into my bedroom, I close the door behind me, grateful she listened so well and hasn't moved from where I planted her on my bed. *Good girl.*

"Everything all right?"

I nod. "We're all set."

She smiles, scooting back on the bed further, an open invitation in her eyes. I close the space to her and sit on the edge of the bed.

My girl doesn't miss a beat, she crawls to me and slides into my lap, straddling me. My hands find her hips once again as an unwelcome sense of uncertainty surfaces. The desire—no, the *need*—to get this right with her overpowers any dick-led impulse.

"We don't have to do anything tonight, Sunshine," I tell her truthfully. "This was only the first date of many."

"Hmm," she hums, toying with the buttons on my shirt as she pops them open slowly. My cock swelling with every slip of her fingers will be my undoing. "I don't think I'd consider this our first date."

My brow furrows. "You don't?"

She shakes her head, sliding her hands down to undo another button. "By my count, I'd call this our...sixth date."

"Sixth?"

Her confident, beaming smile has me entranced as she lists off all our *dates*. "The night you invited me out to the bar to see the band play. The evening you came over to patch my roof and we had dinner." She punctuates each event with a tick of her finger to keep track. "Our hardware store date. Cleaning out the shed. Last night I made dinner and we watched a movie..." She pops her thumb out on her other hand to get her accounted six. "And tonight. Six."

I chuckle. "I don't know if I'd count any of those other occasions as *dates*."

"Well, I do." Her voice is sultry as she pops the last button on my dress shirt, tugging the fabric up and out, exposing my bare chest. Her eyes sparkle as she glides her hands up my arms, over my shoulders, and down my pecs, her nails a lingering promise of what's to come. "And do you know what happens on the sixth date?"

My grip tightens on her hips, guiding her down and grinding her against the hard bar of my engorged length. Her breath hitches and I feel her bear down, the lightest bit of moisture dampening my jeans. "Fuck," I growl, switching my right hand to the back of her head to bring her lips to mine.

Like satin, her lips glide over me, pressing and opening. Her tongue slowly careens over my lower lip and a wave of hot pleasure engulfs me. Kissing her is like winning the fucking lottery.

She moans before nipping my bottom lip. "I have a confession to make," she whispers. Slowly, purposefully, she shifts her weight to ease her legs from my lap to slide down to her delicate knees on the hard floor. I nearly reach out to drag her back to me when she undoes the buckle of my jeans. Her hands are much quicker at work compared to the buttons of my shirt. "Do you want to hear it?"

My mind swims to recall what she said a second ago, too engrossed in watching her confidence bloom before me. "What is it?"

The zipper of my jeans falls and my cock nudges forth as she tugs him free of my briefs. She palms the heated length of me, up and down, cool and soft. I groan.

"I like you," she says just above a whisper, her tongue darting out to taste the head of my cock as she gives it a gentle squeeze, a bead of precum forming on the tip. "A lot."

My chest expands at her admission, knowing I feel the same—if not more toward her. A rushed breath hisses past my lips as she sucks the swollen head into her sweet, hot mouth. Her tantalizing tongue swirling around the crown's edge, sending peaks of pleasure over the sensitive bit of flesh. If I thought her taking my cock in her mouth last night was too good to be true, it's nothing compared to when my girl takes her time like this.

"I like you, too, baby," I moan out pitifully, my hips jerking as she grips the base. "So fucking much," I grunt when I hit the back of her throat. She gags slightly, pulling back before taking me deep again with a low moan in her throat that has me throwing my head back in ecstasy.

My cock leaves her mouth with a wet pop and I bring my gaze back to hers. Pupils dilated, that delicious flush covering her cheeks and part of her exposed chest just begging me to lick and kiss those fuck me lips. Red and swollen with a glisten of her saliva.

When she dives back down for more, I draw back with a chuckle. "You after my cock or my heart, Sunshine?"

She stares up at me with those doe eyes and a teasing smile. And I realize I'm already there. She has it all in the palm of her hand—my heart, my cock. She can have every damn thing I own as long as I get to lay beside her at the end of the day.

"Can't I have both?"

It's those words—those four little words that undo me completely. I reach out, lifting her and pulling her to me a bit rougher than I need to be, but her little gasp and the way she throws herself back on top of me, tells me it's just the right amount. Her mouth lands heavy on mine and we're a tangle of limbs and clothes as I shrug off my shirt and tear off her lacy panties.

"Wha—Butch!"

I chuckle at her outrage as she reaches for the torn scrap of fabric I've lovingly removed and tossed to the side. I grip her chin and turn her focus back to me. "I'll buy you a dozen pairs, if that's what you want," I say. "For now, eyes on me, beautiful."

She sucks her bottom lip between her teeth with a shiver as I lay back on the bed with her on top of me. When she goes to lift her sundress over her head to strip fully, I stop her. "Leave it," I growl, the image of her straddling my face in this sundress has haunted me all evening. Smacking her ass, I nudge her further up my chest. "Get up here. I want that sweet pussy dripping on my face, baby."

Tentatively, she leans over me, crawling like the good girl she is until her lush bare ass is sitting on my chest. I groan at the feel of her, my palms cupping and rubbing over the backs of her thighs and ass.

She looks down at me, unsure. "Are you—"

I tug her thighs to either side of my ears. Her pussy hovering just out of reach. "Sit. Down, Sunshine."

With a moan, she eases down onto my face and immediately I lock my forearm over her thighs, pinning her core to my mouth. I bury my face into her folds—lapping and tonguing her clit. Her legs tremble, and I can feel her try to lift herself, but I refuse to let her go. I continue licking and sucking her delicate nub until she relaxes fully to sit right where she belongs. Probing her entrance with my tongue, I groan deeply as she begins to grind down on me. Her hips jerking and tensing, struggling to hold the handful of her dress at her waist as her pussy flutters over my tongue.

"Mmm," I growl. *That's my good, good girl.*

Her hands dart out, clutching my head and threading through my hair as she gasps and moans out my name. The taste of her slick cunt floods my tongue and mouth. I redouble my efforts as she rides my face, sucking the swollen bit of throbbing flesh between my lips to prolong her orgasm.

My cock jerks against my lower abdomen at the promise of sinking deep in this delicious cunt and making it mine. Precum smears over my oversensitive length and skin.

Dazed, Cassidy lifts on her knees and sits back on my chest. I rub her bare skin anywhere and everywhere I can get my hands on. Kissing the soft insides of her thighs over and over again. "Good girl, Sunshine."

She sucks in a breath and I peer up into her lust-filled eyes, her ready cunt fresh with her release. I can't wait another second. I hook my arms under her thighs and flip her to lay on her back on the mattress.

My girl squeaks, startled before her beautiful laughter graces my ears. I grin as I loom over her, leaning down to tug her breasts free and lavish them with attention. Her hands in my hair, an arch of her back, and a moan on her lips tell me she's more than ready.

I pull away with a wet kiss on her pert nipple and sit back. "If you don't want me ripping this dress, baby, you better get it off now."

She sits up as I slip off the bed to drop my jeans and briefs, kicking them to the side. Her dress lands in a pile on the floor at my feet, causing me to bring my gaze back up to the woman of my dreams lying naked on my bed.

I stand there, like an idiot, burning this moment to memory. How gorgeous she is lying there, waiting for me, ready for me. Ready to become mine in every sense of the word.

I reach toward my bedside table, then hesitate. If I can have it my way, there shouldn't be a single thing between us this first time—or any time in the future. "Do you want to use..."

"Oh, um." Cassidy pauses, glancing between me and the opened drawer. "I'm on the pill, if that's what you—"

I slam the drawer shut, climbing back on the bed to the sound of her giggle. "I'm clean," I say, settling back over her. Her legs loop around my hips as she tugs me down to kiss her. "I haven't been with anyone in...a while."

"Me either," she whispers, leaving light pecks to dust over my lips and cheeks. Her arms circling my neck. "I trust you."

There she goes again, giving me words that mean too fucking much in my mind. It's hard to believe we've finally gotten here, but I'm so fucking glad we did.

With a hand braced beside her head and the other gripping the base of my cock, I angle my hips toward hers. Gliding the already damp head of my cock through her wet heat, we both groan. "You ready, sweetheart?"

She tugs me down over her, lips sealing against mine as she gasps, "Yes."

I push into her slowly, savoring every sensation—every moment we're having together for the first time. Her pussy stretches wide as it flutters around my thick length and clamps down before I'm even fully seated. "Fuck, baby."

I swallow her echoing moan as I thrust hard, needing to give her everything. "Oh-oh, mmm, Butch." She's a panting mess as her inner walls tighten around me, another orgasm washing over her. It's a small one, not like the one I gave her last night or when she sat on my face just now, yet it has my cock weeping for more all the same.

And I fully intend on making her come so hard we both see stars by the end of the night.

Keeping a steady rhythm, I sink deep with every plunge of my cock. Fucking my girl like I know she needs; I start to pound into her. Harder. Faster. On every moan she gives me, I groan and fuck her harder until she's meeting me thrust for thrust. Her heels dig into my ass, nails clinging to my lower back as if she's afraid I'll get up and walk away from her.

Not a chance in hell.

"Cass," I groan, driving into her. Loving the wet slapping sounds coming from between us. The slick satin feel of her cunt is unlike anything.

"You feel so good, Butch," she moans.

I nearly shudder as the slow clench of her pussy around my cock begins to tighten once again. I lift her hips in my hands, her back arching off the bed and changing the angle as I bring her to me—using her, ramming my cock deep within her tight grip.

"Yes, yes, yes—right th-there." Her scream of ecstasy triggers my own release as I pound her onto my cock—once, twice, and on the third, I collapse over her. My cock is seated to the hilt as I come deep inside her hot, soaked cunt with a hiss of her name on my ragged breath.

I don't pull out as I ease us slowly onto our sides, bringing her leg over mine so I can keep my cock right where it belongs. Panting, I kiss her forehead, sliding my arms under her to bring her even closer. "You can have both," I say, kissing her again simply because I can.

She sighs, her head resting on my chest. "Hmm?"

I chuckle at how sated she sounds. "You asked if you could have both before," I murmur, burying my nose in her neck and inhaling deeply. "You can have it all as long as I can have you."

She's quiet for a long moment, only the sound of her quick breath to be heard. Her hand slides up my chest and over my heart, as she tilts her head up. "You have me," she whispers.

I lean in, capturing her lips with mine.

Twenty.

Cassidy

MY TONGUE PEEKS OUT between my lips as I focus my hand on getting the swoop of the trees in the image how I want them.

Butch's loud snore from beside me brings a smile to my face and causes me to lose focus. He's already swatted my pen twice and nudged the tablet out of my hands once when he tugged me closer to him in his sleep.

I peer over at him, his thick, tatted forearm locked over my middle, holding me close. His face buried in the tangled mess of my hair I regret not putting up last night after the second round of...well, you know.

My cheeks heat and I clench my thighs together at the memory.

Last night was amazing. I couldn't have asked for more. It was really, *really* good and so dang hot I saw stars at one point. The level of intimacy and chemistry between us these last few weeks has been rising so quickly...

Then last night happened and it was everything—it *is* everything. Butch Montgomery is my person. I can feel it in my chest and in the way he holds me even now in his sleep, clinging to me like he's afraid I'll disappear.

He makes me feel safe and protected and like I can be myself unapologetically. That wanting to sit at home on a Saturday night and watch old western movies with Frankie is normal and not boring at all. With him, I feel...whole.

Like I'm not so alone in this world anymore.

The thought brings an unwanted tear to my eye. I quickly swipe it away before it can land on Butch's outstretched arm, sniffling quietly to choke back my emotions. I don't even know why I'm getting emotional. I've never been happier than in this moment—quietly working on a small card design while a hunk of a man snores beside me. Holding me close and keeping me warm with his body heat, the early morning sun peeking in through the curtains.

If I could have this kind of morning every day, I'd live a happy life.

"What ya workin' on, babe?" His groggy, sleep-heavy voice meets my ears and I smile at him squinting at the lit screen of my tablet in hand.

"Nothing in particular," I say quietly. "Just playing around."

He grunts, lifting his head just enough to rest it on my upper arm. "Mind showing me what else you've made?"

My heart flutters with warmth. Even though I debate powering down the tablet and telling him *maybe some other time*, I opt to show him all forty-seven cards I have completed. I go through each one, showing him the designs and various color changes. Which ones took me the longest, my favorites, ones I've had printed to give to people. "Alison thinks I should open an online shop and sell them," I say, finally turning off the tablet and setting it on the nightstand.

"Why don't you?" he asks, bringing me closer as I slide deeper under the covers.

I shrug. "I don't know. Seems like a lot of work to turn a hobby into an income, you know?"

His big hand trails gently along my naked back. "Wouldn't be work if it brings you joy," he says, kissing my temple. "Some big names already think you're pretty great."

That's true. *Hallmark* did buy another one of my cards. But that's only two out of the dozens I've submitted. "Maybe," I whisper, snuggling closer in his embrace. "Peggy did tell me I could put in one of those card stands in the coffee shop if I wanted to."

"That'd be a good start," he says sleepily, kissing down my arm and urging me to lay back as his muscular body lifts over me. "After."

I bite back a smile, looping my arms around his neck. "After what?"

He raises a single dark brow, and with a lopsided grin, he dips his head to my bare chest. Leaving light kisses over each breast before licking a slow trail to my nipple.

I squirm under him, arching my back for more as he takes the nipple in his mouth and sucks—hard. "Butch," I gasp.

Frankie's high-pitched whine echoes just outside the closed bedroom door.

Butch pauses and looks up at me. I laugh, gently shoving him away. "Come on," I say, holding the sheet to my chest as I check my phone for the time. I peer over my shoulder at a disgruntled mountain man. "Your girl needs breakfast."

The light that flickers in his eyes at me saying I'm his ignites. He pounces on me, dragging me back under the covers and pinning me down. We're a tangle of limbs and kisses and sheets—laughing and smiling as I wrestle to slip free and get out of bed at some point this morning.

"All right, all right," he mock-grumbles, letting me slip away. He lays back on the pillow, the sheet dangerously low on his hips and his bulge not-so-subtly growing. He watches me pick up my sundress from the floor and tip-toe to the attached bath. "You want to go out for breakfast this morning?"

I leave the door open as I turn on the shower. "I figured I'd grab us something from work and bring it back."

The bed creaks in the other room and his heavy footfalls come closer. I toss my hair up on top of my head, tying it off before stepping into the shower. His wide silhouette frames the doorway as I slide the glass shower door closed behind me. "You have work today?" he asks, not sounding pleased.

"No, but I forgot to bring those contracts Peggy wanted me to look over home with me yesterday," I say as he grabs two towels and places them on the counter. I watch him oddly as the shower door opens and he steps in. "What are you doing?"

"What does it look like? Conserving water." He steps under the showerhead with me, letting it splash over his face with a scrub of his hand.

I snort, bumping him out of the way with my hip and squeezing under the stream of water. "Anyway." I laugh. "I thought I'd pick us up some muffins and breakfast sandwiches while I'm there. Is that okay?"

Those burly hands of his find my ass, hauling me against him. "And what am I supposed to do while you're gone?"

"Wake your brother up. Get him in the shower and a few aspirin for the headache I'm sure he'll have once he gets around. Then I'll bring the coffee," I tell him, reaching around to grab my body wash and squirting out a dollop. "Maybe talk to him? Make sure he's okay after...last night," I add quietly, remembering his reason for the annual drunken stupor.

"He told you?"

I look up at him shaking his head. "I promise I won't tell anyone. His secret is safe with me, I swear."

"No, Sunshine, that's not what I meant," he says with a sigh, helping me to rinse off while taking extra care over my ass and breasts. "You're the first person he's told outside of the family. He hasn't even told any of our other siblings—only my parents and I know."

"Oh…"

"Yeah," he grunts. "And if he told you…well, consider yourself one of the family now."

Despite the grim subject, I can't tamp down the smile creeping in. "That's sweet of you to say."

"I mean it," he adds as I step out, grabbing a towel to dry off. "Which means Sunday dinner tonight is mandatory for you, too."

I laugh at his obvious play considering my uncertainty when he brought it up yesterday. "Fine, fine," I tease. "I'll go with you." I poke my head in the shower. "I'll be back in an hour, tops. Do you want anything else or the usual?"

"I'll try one of those new muffins I saw last week. Dealer's choice," he says through sloshing water, leaning out for a kiss. "Drive safe."

The bell over the front door at Cup O' Joe chimes as I push through. All the tables are taken and there's a line about four customers deep with Janice manning the register and one of the new part-time hires filling orders.

"Hey, you," Alison greets me from behind the display, loading it with a fresh batch of—what Peggy likes to call—*massive* muffins. "What are you doing here? How did it go last night?"

"Great," I say, trying and failing to keep the heat from rising to my cheeks.

So what? I slept with Butch Montgomery last night and I've been steadily falling head over heels for the man for weeks now. We're together. He's made that abundantly clear over the last twenty-four hours—the whole town will find out soon enough, I'm sure. "I just need to grab something from the back. I'm taking breakfast with me, too. What kind are these?"

"Apple cinnamon. How many do you want?" she asks, grabbing a paper bag from under the display.

Peggy lets us eat for free while we're on the clock and generously gives us an employee discount when we're off, so I decide to splurge. "Six," I call behind me, heading for the back office. I grab the copies I made yesterday from the desk and head back to the front to get in line.

"Hey, Cass."

I turn at the sound of my name, my gaze landing on Alex. I fight back an immediate response of something snarky considering how creepy he was acting the last time I saw him at Tavern Nine. But he doesn't smell like beer or piss and for once he appears to be full-blown sober. "Hey."

He takes the open spot in line behind me, pushing his hands in his jean pockets. "You, uh, gotten to talk to Garrett yet?"

My brow furrows. Why would he ask me that? He was there, sitting on the couch at the trailer on Garrett's birthday, not doing a damn thing while Garrett and I argued for hours. "Not in a few days. Why?" Worry slices through me like ice. Did something happen?

He nods solemnly, staring down at his shoes. "I know I haven't exactly had his back, I guess...but I'd like to reach out to him. Let him know I support his decision and whatnot."

"I can help whoever's next in line," Janice calls out.

I step forward, my mind swimming as I relay my order to her before turning back to Alex. "What do you mean by *his decision?*"

He actually has the gall to act uncomfortable, shifting on his feet. "I mean, I get it. It had to be his choice to go, but I—"

I put my hand up, stopping him. "Alex, what are you talking about? Where is my brother?"

"He left," he says. "He sent out a mass text to me and a few of the guys saying he was admitting himself to a rehab facility west of Billings. Said he had some shit to work through and that he couldn't keep going on like he has been."

My heart nearly stops in my chest. He *left*? Without telling me or bothering to say goodbye? "What? When?"

"Yesterday," he tells me. "I asked if he needed a ride, but he said he already had one. That Butch Montgomery was taking him."

He lied to me. I swallow down the heartbreak rising in my throat like bile.

Butch lied to me. He chose not to tell me about Garrett and acted like everything was fine all evening. How could he possibly think that was the right thing to do?

Tears burn my eyes as I pay Janice—who's listening in, of course, with clear surprise of her own marring her face. I gather the food and tray of coffee in my arms.

"If you, uh, get a phone number for the place," Alex says, "I'd really like to talk to him if they'll let me."

I nod, too quickly and too much as tears openly fall, blurring my vision. "Yeah—I mean, yes. I'll...get all the information and let you know."

He thanks me as I hurry out the door and over to my car. I don't know whether to race back to Butch's and slap him for lying to me, for taking my brother away, for not telling me he was planning this. For not letting me say goodbye.

I sob on the ride home. A raging war of anger and fear and hope and gratitude all battle for center stage of my emotions. *Think rationally, Cassidy.* I'm trying, but it's hard to think about anything except my brother is gone to—I don't even know where. *He's all I have left.* But is he? I have Alison and Peggy and Cup O' Joe and...Butch.

I *had* Butch.

I don't know if I have him anymore.

He lied. Did he, though?

Yes. Keeping something from someone you care about, especially something as important as this, is the same as lying.

I pull into the long drive and park beside Butch's truck, killing the engine. I catch a glimpse of my face in the rearview mirror, red and blotchy with tears still streaming down my cheeks. I suppose it's a good thing I didn't bother with makeup before leaving this morning, merely throwing on a tank and sweats, trying to hurry back to spend as much of the day with Butch before dinner at his parents.

My heart hurts and there's a pit a mile wide growing between me and that front door, waiting for me to fall.

With breakfast in hand, I push the door open with my foot and kick it closed behind me with enough force for it to echo throughout the house. Frankie barks, paws scurrying over hardwood in my direction as I set everything down on the island in the kitchen.

There's a groan from the couch—which I don't bother to acknowledge—as Duke's shuffled feet head toward the scent of coffee. "Which one is two creams no sugar?" he asks.

I take a deep breath and turn to him, putting my purse on a hook. How hard is it for people to read a damn lid on a to-go order?

I point and Duke takes the correct cup, sipping it slowly. He peers at me out of the corner of his eye as Butch comes down the stairs freshly showered and dressed for the day; it even appears he trimmed his beard a little.

When his gaze lands on me, whatever smile he had lingering dies. "What happened?" He comes right over to me, reaching out as I step away.

I glance at Duke standing on the other side of the island, unsure if I want to cause a scene in front of his brother—but the hell with it. He's made enough decisions for me lately.

"When the *fuck* were you going to tell me you took my brother to a rehab facility?" There's more bite in my voice than I intended, my anger coming through at the forefront as another sob chokes me.

"Well, that's my cue," Duke mutters, digging in the bag and taking a breakfast sandwich with his coffee in hand as he heads for the door. Frankie is hot on his heels in hopes the hungover man will stumble and drop something good. "Come on, hot dog. Let's go raid your new dad's garage."

The front door slams shut and I'm left alone with one mentally conflicting judgment call.

"How could you not tell me?" I hiss at his frozen frame towering before me. "He's my brother, Butch. *Mine*. You don't get to make those kinds of decisions for me. You didn't even let me say goodbye." I'm full-on sobbing now, the fear of something happening to Garrett that's always lingered in the back of my mind coming forth.

"Sweetheart, I—" He reaches for me again, but I push his hand away. He rubs his face roughly, his eyes darting around like he can't find the words. "It wasn't my call."

I sniffle. "Yes, it was. You took him."

He shakes his head. "No, I mean, yeah, I drove him out there, but he's the one who said he didn't want to see you."

My heart breaks all over again, my lower lip wobbling. "He said that?" Garrett is the one who didn't want to say goodbye? Regret for how I left things the last time I saw him crashes into me like a freight train. I bury my face in my hands, crying. No wonder he doesn't want to see me.

"I t-told him I was done with him," I cry. "And now he h-hates me."

"No, baby, no." Butch swoops in, his arms wrapping around me and pulling me tight against his racing heart. "God, no, Sunshine. It's not you, he just...he needs time to figure his shit out."

"That's what you said before—and now he's gone." My entire body trembles in time with my sobbing little heart. How could I have been so cruel to him?

Butch readjusts, his large hands cupping my cheeks and tilting me up to face him. "Stop," he growls. "He is not gone. He's getting *help*. For you. For himself. He said he couldn't say goodbye to you because it would've kept him from leaving at all. Your brother loves you so damn much, sweetheart, he asked me to take care of you while he's away."

"He did?" I say just above a whispered sniffle. "But—Why did he ask you to take him? How does he know about us?"

His slow grin slides a piece of my heart back into place. "Isn't it obvious, beautiful? You're the only thing that matters to me. You're my Sunshine."

I don't let myself overthink it another second. *This man...* This man standing right in front of me has done nothing but think of *me*, of my needs, for weeks—months. Years, so he claims. I have no reason to not believe him at this moment. It's written all over his face even now.

His eyes dance over my features, his jaw ticking in time with whatever worrisome, stressful thought that passes through.

My anger slowly subsides into understanding. The fear still lingers for my brother, no matter how badly I want to believe that he'll be okay. But the gratitude toward Butch and everything he's done for me—for my family—starts to bloom into something more.

I lift on my toes and tug him down to meet me. Gratefully, he does. Our lips move against each other frantically, showing me the worry I knew I saw in his eyes a moment ago. I can't let him think that one misunderstanding could tear us apart. Not with the way I feel about him.

With my face still cradled in his hands, I fumble with the belt clasping his jeans at his thick-cut waist. The same waist I had my legs wrapped around for the first time only last night. Tears continue to cloud my eyes as I slip my fingers over the cool metal.

Butch groans, breaking our kiss to look into my eyes. His breath heavy with building desire. "As much as I'd love to have you hate fuck me right now, sweetheart." He thumbs away several stray tears from my cheeks, his eyes watching mine. "I need to know you're okay."

I shake my head with a light sniffle. "I'm fine."

"Your eyes and these tears are telling me otherwise, Sunshine."

I laugh. I can't help it. This man is all I've ever wanted, and he's all I'll ever need.

I guide him down to meet me for another slow kiss. "I don't want to hate fuck you," I whisper, feeling like my heart is on the line in this vulnerable moment. "I could never hate you."

He chuckles. "You sure about that? What was it—only a month ago you were calling me Asshole by name."

My lower lip wobbles as the overflow of emotions that's been pulling me this way and that for the last half hour come to fruition.

Butch holds my face in his warm, calloused hands. "Hey now, don't do this to me, baby. I can't stand to see you cry."

Warmth floods my chest, my belly, my heart, and my soul, as realization settles over me like a weighted blanket. "I love you."

I watch his eyes as the three little words of truth spill from my lips.

He blinks, staring at me for so long that I shift my hands to hold his wrists on either side of my face.

Faster than I can comprehend, he's on me, kissing me and hoisting me into his arms. He pushes my legs apart, forcing them to wrap around his waist as my ass plops on the cool granite countertop beside us. When he pulls away, dark eyes on me, I swear, they're glossier than before.

"I have loved you from afar for three years, Cassidy. Three years I've never even let myself hope to hear you say those words to me one day. You have no idea..."

"I love you, Butch Montgomery," I whisper against his lips for good measure, letting the tears freefall. "I love you so much it makes me want to cry."

His smile fills me with so much longing that I draw him closer, needing more of him—all of him. "I love you more, Cassidy Clark. I love you more than anything." He grips the waistband of my sweats and I lean back on my hands, tilting my hips up so he can get them off. They hit the ground with my panties a second later and I'm dragging him back between my spread legs, kissing him as I undo his belt and free his cock from his jeans.

I gasp as his thick fingers toy with the folds of my pussy, slowly circling my clit and dipping into my heat. Pushing his jeans and briefs down past his hips, I tug on the steel bar of his length, replacing his fingers with his cock. "Butch," I moan, rubbing the head of his cock up and down my dampening core.

He bucks forward, his silken rod nudging my clit. "That's it, baby. Use me. Get that pussy good and wet for me."

I moan at the feel of him against me, my core slickening at his command. The need to bury him inside me rises with every passing second. When his head dips to my neck, kissing and nipping just below my ear—*my favorite spot*—I position him at my entrance. He pushes in, nice and slow, but that's not what I want from him.

I grip his lower back, digging my nails in as I force him forward. He groans, slamming his thick cock deep. I suck in a breath as he begins to fuck me without restraint.

"Yes, yes, yes." My voice is a chanting moan as he hooks one muscular forearm under my leg and brings me to the edge of the counter.

I hold on for dear life as he pounds me into oblivion. His other hand snakes up my neck and grabs a fistful of hair, forcing my mouth to his. I bite down on his lower lip, sucking it between my lips as the walls of my core begin to flutter with an impending release.

"Fuck," he growls, tugging my head back and burying his face in my neck as his hips pound against my ass. The echoing wet slaps heighten the moment to a degree I didn't think was possible. "Say it again," he demands, punctuating his words with a hard thrust. "Tell me you love me. Tell me to never let you go. Say it. Say you're fucking *mine*."

I moan, gasping for the crest of release. "I-I'm yours. Oh, Butch..."

My orgasm crashes through me with a tight clamp of my pussy around his driving cock and a cry of his name. His hold on my neck and leg stiffens as he rams into me with a shudder, stilling his thrust and spilling his release deep inside.

My arms find purchase wrapped around his strong neck as he repositions me on the counter, not realizing he had lifted me off it at some point.

"I'm sorry," he pants, breathless. "I should've told you sooner. I shouldn't have listened to him when he said not to tell you he asked for help."

I sigh, resting my head against his broad chest and listening to his heartbeat. "Don't be. You did everything right," I admit. And it's true. He could've told me last night, but now that I think about it...

I wouldn't change a thing because it might not have ended how it did—us sleeping naked together and confessions of *like* that were teetering dangerously close to *love* were admitted. "I'm sorry I blew up on you."

My chin rests on his chest, peering up at him as his hands do my new favorite thing—gliding soothingly up and down my spine.

"It's good to know what to watch out for now," he teases as my brow furrows in confusion. He chuckles. "If I hear an f-bomb drop from these pretty lips again, I'll know I'm in big trouble."

I throw my head back with a laugh. I suppose he's not wrong there.

"Is it safe to come in now?" Duke's voice carries from the front door just barely out of view from where we're still, *ahem*, joined.

"No!" Butch barks back, earning a giggle from me. The security I feel in his arms as he shifts me to turn his back toward the short entry hall, shielding me as best he can, is everything.

His eyes snap to meet mine as I purposefully clench his dick still buried balls deep in my all too pleased pussy. "Mind conserving some more water with me, love?"

He grins, lifting me in his arms. "Always."

Twenty-One.

Butch

"ARE YOU SURE?" CASSIDY asks, biting her lip as she surveys the wide selection spread out at the local in-store bakery. "I thought you said Levi hates nuts."

"He'll live," I grunt.

She glares up at me disapprovingly. And I'm a sucker for that little scrunch in her nose she does when she's annoyed. "Just because *you* want the pecan pie doesn't mean *everyone* wants the pecan pie."

The smile that splits my face has her looking more and more flustered. Tugging her into my arms in the middle of the cake and pie section of the bakery, I kiss her temple. "Fine. We'll get the pecan *and* the apple. Sound good?"

"No," she mutters, tipping her chin up and pecking my lips before turning back to the same array of desserts. "You said your mom asked for two pies. Which, to me, means she wants two of the *same* kind so we can all enjoy it together."

"But…" I sound like a whiny little bitch right now, but in my defense, this pecan pie looks damn good.

"I'll tell you what," she says, setting two apple pies in our basket and taking my hand. Her delicate, soft fingers thread through my rough, burly ones as she steers us away from my pecan pie. "My grandma had an old pecan pie recipe she used to make for my dad on Thanksgiving. I'll see if I can find it in the notebook we brought home yesterday."

It's been a week since Cassidy and I had our first *sort of fight*, as she likes to call it. Unfortunately, last week's Sunday dinner got canceled since my nephew, Parker, was sick with a stomach bug. They didn't want to give it to everyone since he and Lily are living there, too. Solid call, in my opinion. It gave me the day to focus on my girl and make sure she knew how much I loved her.

And I made sure I was very, *very* thorough in clearing any lingering doubts in her mind as to where we stand.

It ended with us making some big decisions. Together. Like cleaning out her trailer in Whitetail Park and moving all of her belongings to my house—*our* house. She's still hesitant to sell it, given her brother will need a place to stay once he finishes rehab, but we all agree that might not be the best move for him.

After seeing how upset Cass had been about not being able to speak to her brother, I was thankful the place I chose to take Garrett allows him to communicate via email with his family and friends. He told us he'll be sending a video chat next week to give proof of life and that he really is doing better.

So, for now, the trailer is cleaned out until he decides what he wants to do—whether that's come back to Whitetail or find some other new horizon to set his sails for. Either way, Cassidy is with me now, and that won't be changing. Ever.

"You told me you can't bake worth a shit," I say as we walk hand in hand.

"Well... I did say that, didn't I." She giggles, stopping to open one of the foggy freezer doors and peering inside. "You'll help me, though, right?" she asks all too sweetly as she plops a tub of French vanilla ice cream in the basket.

As if I could deny spending time with her? Or anything, for that matter.

"Cassidy?"

We both turn, a familiar face standing a few steps away. I recognize her from the bar the night I beat the shit out of Colt for laying a hand on my girl.

"Oh, hi, Madison," Cass greets her, and the tense shift in both of them has me on edge. Their last interaction, as far as I know, didn't go so hot.

Madison glances up at me with an awkward wave. "Hi, Butch."

I grunt, wrapping a protective arm around Cassidy and tucking her into my side.

She catches the hint, lowering her gaze before returning her attention to Cass. "I, um..." Tears spring to her eyes and now suddenly *I'm* the uncomfortable one. "Sorry, this is just harder than I thought it'd be."

Cassidy sighs, stepping toward her and allowing Madison to hug her. She starts rambling quickly between her hiccups and cries, and I can only catch pieces of it. "You were right...I'm so stupid. Please forgive me...I've been trying to get in touch with you for over a week now, but you have me blocked on everything...not that I blame you."

Cass pulls away and steps back beside me, slipping her hand in mine. "Yeah, I've been...busy."

Madison nods. "Totally fair, but...I was wondering if you wanted to hang out tonight, if you're free?"

"We've got plans tonight," she replies, and my chest swells at her including me in that statement. I glare at Cassidy's friend—or old friend, I'm not quite sure—daring her to say anything negative about us being together. But she simply nods yet again, gazing between the two of us.

"Right, of course." Madison takes out her phone from her back pocket. "Can I...text you, then?"

"How about I text you? Since I still have you blocked." Cassidy gives my hand a firm squeeze.

"Let's get going, beautiful," I say, catching on. "We don't want to be late." The women exchange a *goodbye* and *talk soon*, but from the tone my girl says it in, I'm getting the impression she won't be talking to her anytime soon.

Back in my truck, with two apple pies and a container of ice cream sitting in a bag at Cassidy's feet, we're on our way to my folks' place. I spare a brief glance at her gazing out the window, fidgeting with her phone in hand. "What's on your mind, darlin'?"

She sighs, her shoulders dropping. "Is it wrong if I decide not to unblock Madison? I mean, we were best friends for so long...I just don't know if I can forget everything that's happened."

I gather she's referring to her ex and the scene at the bar, but I wouldn't doubt there's even more to the story I wasn't present for. "Your call," I tell her. "But if she doesn't bring anything good into your life, then what's the point?"

Her light laughter has me glancing between her and the road. "What?"

"Nothing." Her tone is teasing as she rests her hand over mine that's been planted on her upper thigh since we got in the truck. "I love you."

Music to my ears. "I love you, too, baby," I say, pressing my thumb into the bare skin of her thigh as my hand eases a slow path upward. My fingers graze over the denim of her shorts and the heat radiating from the apex of her thighs has me groaning. "Remind me again why you decided not to wear the sundress you had on earlier."

She laughs, nudging my hand away. "Because of this exact reason," she teases. "And I know it's your favorite." *Damn right, it is.* "I can't have you distracting me while I'm trying to make a good impression on your family."

I scoff for the hundredth time over her continued concern they won't like her. It's wild to me she thinks anyone could dislike her. "You're with me, Sunshine. Trust me, they'll love you," I say, turning down the long drive of my parents' property stationed about a mile down the mountain from my place.

She readjusts in her seat, leaning forward as the trees part to reveal the place I grew up. The white, mountainside farmhouse with oak accents sits facing the west, complete with a wraparound porch. It's been pictured in several *Country Home* magazines and is the object of my mother's Christmas decorating obsession during the holidays.

"What if they don't?" Cassidy's whispered question has me stopping the truck before getting to the end of the driveway.

I throw the truck in park and turn to her. When she lifts those same doe eyes that hooked me over three years ago, I say, "I don't care what they think. Haven't I made that clear? No one else matters now but you." She opens her mouth to argue my point, I'm sure, but I press on. "Sure, I care about my family and all that, but *you*, Sunshine, *you* are my priority. Whether they like you or not doesn't change the fact you're mine."

She nods weakly, meeting me over the center console. We kiss, soft and slow, until she sits back with a sigh. "Promise?"

A loud, long hold of a car horn blares from behind, causing Cassidy to jump.

I scowl, glaring in the rearview at Levi and Rhett carpooling in Levi's piece of shit Ford. He waves, honking the horn several times in quick bursts. *Idiot.*

"You know I do," I grunt, shifting the truck out of park and pulling into the spot beside Duke's work truck before killing the engine. "And if any one of my dipshit brothers says anything to make you doubt how fucking incredible you are, you better damn well tell me." I try to keep some of the bite out of my tone, but the very idea she could change her mind about me—about *us*—isn't something I want in my head.

Duke's already given his stamp of approval on Cass. Beau isn't even stateside and I haven't spoken to him in easily three months since he got shipped overseas for his third tour. Rhett's head is on straight, but the guy can't learn to mind his own fucking business. Levi might as well be crowned the town's idiot playboy. And Lily can be a real bitch when she wants to be.

Damn. This might not be a good idea after all.

Her soft touch and sultry voice bring me back from starting this truck back up and throwing it in reverse. "Don't go getting anxious on me," she says teasingly. "Only one of us is allowed to have anxiety at a time."

I chuckle, swiftly kissing her before pushing my door open. "Then let's go."

Taking the bag from her hands, I introduce her to my brothers, Rhett and Levi, as they come up behind us. It may be a small town, but Cassidy mentioned she doesn't *know* them in any context of the word. Just knows *of* them.

Funny how the small-town gossip train can still be so lacking in the details when it's everyone's favorite pastime.

Cassidy takes my free hand, gripping it tightly as I lead us up to the porch. The moment the front door flies open, it's a barrage of hellos and hugs from my parents and siblings with Cassidy at the center of it all. At first, her eyes widen and cheeks flush at the overwhelming welcome to the point I worry I may have to haul her away just to let her breathe.

"You can call me Julie," my mother tells her, releasing her from a tight embrace. "Or Mom, whatever you like. And this is my husband, Clayton."

My father shakes Cassidy's hand. "I'd prefer Clayton, calling me *Mom* feels too formal."

I shake my head with a chuckle, as do my brothers. Our father has always been either a hard-ass or a jokester. There's never been much of an in-between with him.

Cassidy wins over my father immediately with a genuine burst of laughter she gives his lame dad joke. And my mother snatches the grocery bag from my hand and whisks my girl away into the house. We all follow her lead, heading inside where it's easy to see Ma went overboard. Yet again.

"Good one bringing your woman, Butch." Levi claps me on the back with a laugh. "We'll be eatin' good tonight."

Duke comes out from the dining room, a scowl on his face. "That's no shit. I made the mistake of showing up early. Ma had me dusting before I could get my damn shoes off."

I grin. My mother's always been big on first impressions—I suppose she and Cass have that in common—and it warms my heart she's going above and beyond to make Cassidy feel welcome. The sound of her laughter alongside the chatter from my mother and sister has my feet moving in her direction.

"Uncle Butts," Parker shouts, barreling toward me.

I catch him around the waist, tossing him as high as I can get him without hitting the ceiling—much to my sister's shouts of protest. I perch my three-year-old nephew on my shoulder and round the large central island in the kitchen toward Cassidy, smiling up at us.

"Did he just call you Uncle *Butts*?" She laughs, beaming the joy I knew she would.

This has been his thing lately, changing everyone's name and giving them close nicknames to the real thing. I'm Uncle Butts, Duke is Duck, Levi is Jeans, and I'm pretty sure Rhett is still Rhett since Parker hasn't figured out a silly name for him yet.

"Parker, do you know who this is?" I ask him, bouncing him down to my forearm as he giggles incessantly.

"Nooo."

"Yes, you do." Lily smiles at her son, chopping cucumbers alongside my mother as she takes the roast out of the oven. "Do you remember her name?"

"Uncle Butts' lady," he says, cracking up with laughter.

"Damn right, she is," I announce proudly, tickling him and earning well-deserved favorite uncle rights for the rest of the night.

The whole evening goes by too fast. Cassidy molds into every conversation seamlessly, talking and laughing. Telling my father exactly how she got the forty-gallon water heater into the tiny utility closet at her trailer by herself.

She's a perfect fit right beside me as I tug her chair until it's touching my own. Wrapping my arm around the back of her chair, she leans into me, resting her head on my shoulder. "Having fun, Sunshine?" I ask, kissing her forehead as my thumb draws lazy circles over her hip.

"I am," she whispers, tilting her chin up to look at me. "Your family is amazing."

I bite back the urge to say, *they're yours now, too*, and settle for, "I'm glad you think so, sweetheart." My murmured words and overabundance of PDA don't get lost on my brothers, who are smirking and whispering to one another across the table as they watch us.

I flip Levi the bird when he mock smooches in our direction like the toddler he is. You wouldn't know he's almost thirty with the way he acts. He's worse than Parker.

"Butch Robert Montgomery, put your hand down," my mother scolds me, earning a booming laugh from my brothers and a snicker from my girl.

I grip Cassidy's luscious hip firmly in my grasp before tugging on one of the belt loops of her shorts. She nudges me playfully and—despite being surrounded by my family—my cock thickens in my jeans. A low rumble rises in my chest only for her to hear.

This woman has no idea what she does to me.

"Cassidy, would you be a dear and get the dessert," Ma says, gathering dishes to clear the table. Lily helps Parker finish his dinner while Levi and Duke join in to clear the table.

"Of course," she says, swatting my hand away and standing.

I can't help but grin, watching her ass as she heads for the kitchen.

"Congratulations." My father's tone is taunting as I turn to him, a smirk on his lips. He leans back in his chair, lifting his chin toward the direction Cassidy just walked in. "I see you've found your Sundance, son."

The joke he's making isn't lost on me, but the implication has me holding my breath. He's right. I've found my partner in this life—or, partner in crime, as my father would say. She's everything I've dreamed of and more. I don't doubt there's anything we can't make it through. And I've never been more sure of anything in my life.

"Ice cream, ice cream," Parker chants, nearly jumping out of his seat as Cassidy returns with dessert.

When she takes her seat beside me, I can't stop myself from planting a heavy kiss on those lips I get to call mine. Dazed, she pulls back with a slow smile. "What was that for?"

"Just making sure," I say, holding her close as my mother begins to plate dessert for everyone.

"I love you," Cassidy whispers.

"I loved you first," I say in return.

Her light, airy laughter is a balm to my soul. She's my Sunshine in this world. And I'm the lucky bastard who gets to call her mine.

Epilogue.

Cassidy

Three months later...

"Oh, my god. Are you seeing this?" I say out loud, unable to believe my eyes.

When Butch came home early last week and found Frankie stuck on the counter in the kitchen, crying for help, he couldn't fathom how he did it. I tried to tell him he's been doing this for years. Ever since my father passed, he's been forced to take walks and eat healthy—god forbid I keep him alive and well for as long as I can.

Butch was so shocked, however, he decided to put up cameras to catch him in the act.

And we're finally watching the video evidence of how the heck he does it.

We watch as Frankie paces near the corner cabinet and begins nudging the double-hinged door. Slowly, he pries it open just enough for him to lift on his hind legs and turn the very top shelf of the rev-a-shelf (Lazy Susan) to create a stepping area for himself by turning the shelves accordingly. The little trickster then pushes off and—after a few low tumbles—he gets his footing and hops from the top inner shelf to the counter.

And, with the momentum to get him up, the shelf spins back to its original setting beneath him and the partially open cabinet door slowly eases shut. Trapping him on the counter until help arrives.

"He's a damn Houdini." Butch chuckles, shaking his head and giving Frankie a rub between the ears. "Did you have one of these shelves at the trailer, too?"

I nod, still at a loss for words as Butch replays the footage. "Yes," I confirm. "There were a few times the cabinet door would be open when I came home and found him, but I never put two-and-two together. I always thought he got it open from trying to get down."

"Well, mystery solved," he says, closing the app on his phone and setting Frankie down. "Looks like we'll be picking up some cabinet locks on the way home tonight."

I laugh. "I guess so."

Butch grabs the basket of goodies for our little impromptu date day as I put Frankie on his leash. I was rather surprised when he suggested having a picnic up on the mountain this afternoon. He claims he found an amazing little spot high up on the ridge when he was passing through to the work site for next season.

I make sure to bring an extra sweater for myself and a small blanket for our little Houdini. With it being mid-September, the weather is cooling down fast. It's my favorite time to go out on the mountain and take in the stunning views. Fall never disappoints in Montana.

On the drive up, Butch lets Frankie sit in his lap until the road gets a bit too bumpy and he needs both hands to get where we're going. Holding an excited little sausage in my arms, we finally stop in a dense part of the woods. There are a few pathways leading in at least three different directions, and I'm a bit nervous. Locals or not, anyone can get lost out here.

"You sure you remember where this place is?" I hate even asking, given Butch is a mountain man through and through. I set Frankie down at my feet before gathering the blankets and closing the truck door behind me.

Butch comes around the back with the basket in hand, tilting his chin to the path closest to us. "Yep. It's right over here. Few minute walk at the most."

I follow his lead as Frankie sniffs all over the place, his tail lashing behind him in excitement for our little adventure. A few minutes later the trees part to the cliffside and the view has me gasping in awe at the sight.

The rich, lush forest of oak and pine extends as far as the eye can see, filled with bold fall colors of orange, red, and yellow with dots of deep green throughout. All leading to the most stunning view of the mountains I have ever seen. It's mid-day, yet there's still a misty fog winding through the trees high up on the surrounding peaks.

"Here. Let me take that," Butch says, breaking my trance over this view as he takes the blanket from my hand and lays it out on a flat section of stone and dirt.

Frankie waddles a little too close to the edge of a fairly steep drop-off, so I tug him back. "Be careful, buddy. You don't have enough cushion to save you from a fall like that."

I sit down on the blanket, folding my legs under me as Butch hands me a treat for Frankie. He waddles over and plops in my lap to enjoy his snack accompanied by the serene views.

"So," he grunts, kneeling beside me. "What do you think?"

I beam a smile up at him before turning my head back to the mountains. "I love it. I can't believe you found this place. Usually, spots like this are riddled with tourists."

"Yeah, I guess you could say I got pretty lucky in finding exactly what I wanted."

My brow furrows and I turn to ask him what he means by that—when all the breath in my lungs escapes me in a gasp.

Butch's dark eyes are on me, watching as I take in him beside me on one knee with a little black box in hand. "Sunshine—"

Oh my god.

"—I have loved you from afar for longer than I care to admit," he says, a handsome smile creeping to his lips. "You make me better than I ever could be without you. I love you more than anything and it would be an honor to call you my wife. Cassidy Marie Clark, will you marry me?"

He opens the small box in his hands, revealing a gorgeous, sparkling round-cut diamond sitting on a white gold band.

"Butch, I—" Tears spring to my eyes as I quickly shift Frankie from my lap and get on my knees in front of my future husband. "Yes," I finally say. "A thousand times, yes!" I throw myself in his embrace and cling to him as pure joy envelops me. "I love you."

"I love you, too...my Sunshine," he whispers, a broken note in his voice as I pull away to witness the few tears of a hardened mountain man break free. He grins wildly at me and I smile in return.

Frankie wiggles his way between us, wanting to be a part of the moment as Butch plucks the ring from the box and slips it onto my finger.

This is the happiest moment of my life.

The first of many to come.

The End.

Thanks for reading!
Please leave a review on Amazon or Goodreads to let me know what you thought!

Don't forget to sign-up for my newsletter <u>HERE</u> and receive your *FREE* copy of *Only by You*, the insta-love story of Clayton & Julie, prequel novella to Montgomery Brothers of Montana!

Ready for more Montgomery brothers? Keep reading for a sneak
peek of Duke's story in Found by You,
Book Two: Montgomery Brothers of Montana

XO,
A. Boss

Found by You

Duke

"We're having a baby!" Cassidy, my brother Butch's fiancée, announces over dinner at my parents.

My chest tightens.

My mother, Julie, leaps from her seat to hug Cassidy, then Butch. "Oh, my baby is having a baby," she coos, tears in her eyes.

Butch and Cassidy have been living together for nearly four months now. It was a mere month ago when my brother finally mustered up the courage and asked Cassidy to marry him.

If I thought the idea of attending my brother's wedding hurt... It doesn't compare to this.

I should be happy for them. I *need* to be happy for them, but it's so fucking hard when I had it all and lost it in a blink of an eye that was in the shape of a plane crash.

Four years ago, that same blink took the love of my life, my high school sweetheart, my wife, Rachel...along with our unborn child.

She was only six weeks at the time. We hadn't even announced it to our families yet. Rachel wanted to wait until the first doctor's appointment before we made any kind of announcement. She was on her way to visit her sister in Billings, eager for her be the first one to know.

Then the plane went down—engine failure, they told me—taking the lives of all four on board.

It took five, if you ask me.

Being a father was a silent dream of mine. Silent to those around me, but not to her. Rachel and I knew we wanted kids. *A crap ton.* Her words, not mine. And I was all for it. Kids weren't a hard sell, I wanted them just as bad, if not more.

Now...five years later, she's still gone, and I'm still alone.

I've bought the neighboring property between my brothers, Butch and Beau, right up the road from our folks' place. I even started building my dream home with the help of my other brothers, Rhett and Levi, a few months ago.

Moving on with my life these last few years has been hard in itself, planning for the future has brought a whole different kind of hurt I didn't anticipate when I started this endeavor four months ago when I put my house up for sale.

I'm currently renting out one of Beau's vacation rental cabins on his mountain side property. He's got two built at the moment, and since being stationed overseas for the last eighteen months, my parents and siblings all help with maintenance and booking them on his behalf.

There's five of us Montgomery sons. All of us owning and operating our own business. If there's one thing people know from the last name Montgomery, it's that we don't do anything half assed—I sure as hell didn't.

Montgomery Repair & Towing. I eat, breathe, and sleep my business. Trucks, cars, the occasional motorcycle and boat—I fucking *live* for the classic shit. Old, new, and everywhere in between. We're the #1 go-to repair shop in all of Whitetail, Montana and the three surrounding counties. I've built a solid standard with my reputation.

Butch and I are close, being a year apart and looking like damn twins, we were basically raised as such. Beau's always been the loner of the siblings, straight laced with a stick up his ass eighty-percent of the time. Leaving Rhett and Levi close enough to start their company together.

But when it comes to the big events, we always make it about the group. And now with a wedding and a baby on the way...the Montgomery's are only growing.

"Congratulations," my father, Clayton, chimes in, giving the soon-to-be parents a hug of his own.

Butch gives me a concerned glare at my silence and I take the cue, doing my damnedest to keep my voice even despite the unwanted emotions building inside of me. "Congratulations, guys."

Rhett and Levi give their own cheers, and as the conversation shifts to talk about the baby and due date—all I hear is *six weeks*—and I cringe.

I physically cringe because I can't help myself. The memories are subtle, fading by the day, but that feeling I had when Rachel told me she was pregnant...

That's a feeling I'll never forget.

"So, what you're saying is, the night Butch proposed...he decided to give you a little...early wedding gift?" Lily laughs.

Cassidy nods, beaming a smile with happy tears in her eyes. "I guess so."

Butch scoffs, wrapping his arm around Cassidy and pulling her close to his side. When he kisses her on the temple, I decide it's time to go.

"Well, thanks for dinner, Ma," I say, standing from my seat, "but I've got some late snow plowing to get done if I plan on opening the shop on time tomorrow."

My mother gives me a hard look, and I already know I'll hear shit about this from her on the phone tomorrow. Going around the table, I say my goodbyes. When I reach Cassidy, I give her a long hug as she whispers, "Are you okay?"

I nod, clearing my throat as I pull away from her. "Congrats again, guys. Can't wait for the little shit kicker to get here."

She smiles weakly as Butch lifts his chin, standing. "I'll walk you out."

I head to the front door of my parents' old farm house. It's gone through a few renovations over the years with the help of my siblings, but it still holds its rustic country charm. A family home, through and through.

One I hope to emulate someday.

Yanking on my steel toed boots and Carhartt jacket, I walk outside with Butch hot on my heels. *And he thinks I'm the annoying one.*

"We were going to tell you first," he says. "But, uh, you've been so busy lately. No one's really seen you around."

"Don't worry about it," I say, reaching my blacked-out company wrapped truck with *Montgomery Repair & Towing* written in a bold silver and harsh red with a steel plow on the front. "I'm happy for you guys. You deserve this, Butch."

He pushes his hands in his pockets, eyeing me as I hop in the driver's seat. "So do you, ya know," he huffs, forcing a cloud of steam from his nostrils into the cold mid-December night. "That's what you told me, isn't it? If even a prick like me can find it, you can find it again."

My jaw tightens, my resolve crumbling to mere ash. "And what if I don't want to find it again, Butch, huh? No woman I've met for the last four years has changed a goddamn thing for me. I'm done looking, all right? I'll do ya one better, I'll be the brother who dies alone on this fuckin' mountain. How's that sound? Cause it sounds damn good to me," I bite out, slamming the door as I start my truck.

Butch goes to grab the door, but I lock it. He bangs on the window, trying to tell me something about *not leaving like this,* but I ignore him and peel out down the snowy driveway.

The last person I'll be taking any kind of relationship advice from is one of my damn brothers.

Get ready for Duke's second chance at love in
Found by You,
Book Two: Montgomery Brother of Montana!
Sign up for my newsletter at abossauthor.com and receive the FREE,
insta-love story of Clayton & Julie, prequel novella to Montgomery
Brothers of Montana!

Note from the Author

Thank you for choosing to pick up this book and read it! It means so much to me that you chose to spend your time reading something that I wrote. If I could hug you through this page, I would.

I hope you loved this enough to come back for more, because I certainly intend to put more out in the world from the *Boss Babe Universe*!

Don't forget to sign-up for my newsletter <u>HERE</u> and receive your *FREE* copy of *Only by You*, the insta-love story of Clayton & Julie, prequel novella to Montgomery Brothers of Montana!

Are you a *Boss Babe*?

Join the *Boss Babe Universe* on Facebook, Twitter/X, and Instagram!

About the Author

A. Boss proudly proclaims to be a romance enthusiast who just loves love! When she's not diligently spilling her heart and soul into a word document, you'll find her hanging out with her loving husband, two crazy kids, and two sleepy dachshunds.

You can follow her on all the social media platforms for updates, freebies, and sneak peeks at upcoming releases. Twitter/X, Facebook, Instagram – whatever your poison may be – drop by and say hello!

Everyone is welcome in the *Boss Babe Universe*!

Acknowledgements

A huge thank you to my critique ladies and beta readers – Sarah, Leah, Colleen, Sevannah, Valerye, and Jeanette – I appreciate all of you!

To Jill – for being my own personal cheerleader over the years. You're the best!

And to Danika Bloom, founder of Author Ever After, for your endless support and ability to answer any question thrown at you. Thank you!